Short Horror Stories
Supernatural Suspense Collection
Volumes 1 & 2
Written by Ron Ripley, Sara Clancy, Rowan Rook,
and David Longhorn
Edited by Kathryn St. John-Shin

ISBN: 9781705822982
Copyright © 2019 by ScareStreet.com

Thank You and Bonus Novel!

We'd like to take a moment to thank you for your ongoing support. You make this all possible! To really show you our appreciation for purchasing this book, we're giving away one of our full-length horror novels. **We'd love to send you a full-length horror novel in 3 formats (MOBI, EPUB and PDF) absolutely free!** This will surely make chills run down your spine!

Download your full-length horror novel, get free short stories, and receive future discounts by visiting www.ScareStreet.com

See you in the shadows,
Team Scare Street

Table of Contents

Volume 1

Let's Play
By Rowan Rook

Emmie left the lights out for a few minutes longer. With the computer asleep and the door sealed, the recording room was as silent as the inside of a coffin. The acoustic foam dampened sound from the outside world and buried her in like feet of soil. Her hush magnified her shaky breath.

"Shit."

Her fingers dug into her sweaty, aching brow. She couldn't say how long she'd sat like that, slumped into her computer chair. She was almost certainly late for the live stream but she couldn't bring herself to check the clock.

It's not my fault, she repeated to herself.

"Dead from a Broken Heart: Super-Fan EmmShadow Commits Suicide After Rejection by Gamer-Girl Idol," the tabloids had written, their lurid headlines laid out like webs to ensnare the same sort of person EmmShadow himself had been: trolls, GamerGaters, creeps.

He was no fan, she reminded herself. *He was a stalker.*

She dreaded checking her email every morning—for every good-hearted letter from a fan thanking her for cheering them up with her videos or inspiring their daughter to pursue a STEM field, there was a threat against her family for 'making money off men's hearts online' by 'being a fake geek-girl,' a promise to stalk every Starbucks in Seattle in search of her, or an unsolicited nude photo of some generic, pasty harasser. But as bad as her online messages were, the letters she'd found slipped beneath her door were something else altogether. Each declaration—demand—of so-called love had been signed 'EmmShadow,' a name she'd seen tied to crude remarks all over her comments sections and fan pages online. When she'd gotten the police involved, they hadn't found him. When she'd posted her response online in the form of a video condemnation of her stalker, however, the results had been very different.

One more letter had invaded her home: a photograph of his face. She could still see it burned onto the back of her lids. A blank smile. His blue eyes narrowed but clear. His teeth bared but perfectly aligned. His lips straight but calm. His brown bangs swept across clammy cheeks. "Come with me," he'd written on the back. "You'll get what you deserve."

The next day, a man was found hanged in his Tacoma home. In his suicide note, he'd confessed to being EmmShadow and claimed he couldn't have continued living after his "soulmate's" condemnation.

The tide of hate was swift and brutal—entitled men and EmmShadow sympathizers calling her a murderer for daring to stand up for herself against a supposed fan. While so many subscribers and generally reasonable people saw through the headlines, the bile strewn toward her through the cloud had kept her away from her ZTube channel for almost two weeks. Her Let's Play videos were her only source of income. She needed to get back into the game, for herself and for all the people who supported her. One dead creep had no right to get to her this much. He was gone; she was safe.

"I can do this," she promised herself aloud. "It'll be just like any other live stream."

Then she flipped on the spotlights. The too-bright glow throbbed in her temple, but she ignored it, wiping her sweaty hands on her jeans and swiping her computer's mouse to wake up the machine. She checked her reflection in the dim screen as it booted up, making sure her trademark smile was in place and her black bangs didn't stick to her brow.

She tried to chuckle, "The show must go on."

When she signed into ZTube, she was 12 minutes late for her

scheduled live stream.

"Where is she?" comments asked in the live chat.

"Too scared to show her face again after what she's done."

"She's messing with you—you're all wrapped up in her web, just like EmmShadow. Pathetic."

Her stomach churned. She let her eyes catch on better comments—"I hope she's okay," "She doesn't have to do this if she isn't ready," "We miss you, Emmie!"—before taking a deep breath and turning on her webcam. Her face appeared in the corner of her screencast video. A pulse of adrenaline switched her into the performer's mindset she'd practiced over the years of building a career out of her channel.

"Hello, geeks and gamers!" She pulled her mic close and followed her script. "I hope you haven't missed me too much." She hid her shudder. "As I'm sure all of you know, it's been something of a rough two weeks, but I don't want to dwell on that. Neither do you. You're here for a little healthy escapism, so let's get to it."

She clicked on her desktop, navigating to the folder where she'd downloaded the game she planned on playing. Normally, she was more prepared than this.

"Before we get started, I just want to say thank you to all of you who have stuck by me." She forced herself to stare directly into the camera and pretended that several thousand people weren't staring back. "It's not easy being a public figure online, but those of you who earnestly enjoy my videos for what they are make it all worth it." Sometimes, she wondered if that were true— if she wouldn't have been better off becoming a lawyer like her parents wanted—but she didn't say so aloud.

"Love you, Emmie!" popped up in the chat and caught the corner of her eye. Her lips twitched with a more genuine smile.

"I've got a treat for you today," she announced. "I'm finally going to take a shot at We Remain. We could all use a little adventure, huh?"

Exclamation marks lit up the live chat.

She double-clicked the game's file and its title screen swallowed up her desktop. The full name—We Remain in the Dark—stretched across a black background in a bright red pixelated font. Faux 8-bit tones chimed out an appropriately ominous theme song. Despite its low budget and retro-stylings, the indie horror game had been the latest craze to sweep ZTube during her absence. Almost every other major streamer had already given it a go. The sort of people who enjoyed Let's Plays never seemed to get enough of giggling while their favorite ZTubers shouted and startled. She told herself it was good-natured catharsis.

"Thanks to my recent media blackout, I don't know much about this game going in," she admitted. "I hope it gets a few good screams out of me."

She pressed Start.

***

Squares of rain sprayed out blue pixels when they hit the ground. The game's stick-figure protagonist meandered up what appeared to be a mountain road—it was hard to tell with such blocky graphics—toward the outline of an old house with darkened windows.

The game's prologue had suggested Emmie was playing as a bereaved teen searching for a missing sister—a missing sister who had come to this creepy, isolated, and apparently abandoned manor to marry her lover only to never be heard from again. Emmie paused to make a few witty—she hoped—comments about the absurdity of the situation. The words flowed easily from her mouth but barely registered in her mind. She only hoped the game wouldn't make her think too hard. A few wisecracks, a few exaggerated shouts, then she could call it good and curl back up in bed.

She pressed the arrow keys to move her character forward. Digital stairs let out ugly, distorted creaks as she climbed the porch and approached the front door. Her character knocked after a tap on the ENTER key.

"Why are you here?" appeared in red text when a shadow peeked through the locked door's small window.

Two choices popped up: *"I'm here to save my sister"* or *"I'm here to save myself."*

She tilted her head at the second option. A commentary about grief, perhaps? About the protagonist wanting to save themselves the pain of loss? A bit pretentious for such a simple game. She made a few absentminded comments as such to her viewers before selecting the first choice.

"Liar," accused the figure on the other side of the door. *"Either way, you may make the choice to try, but you will not succeed."*

The digital door clicked open and exposed a sliver of black from within the house. Her character stood on the porch, waiting for her command. She stepped inside.

With the crash of the door slamming behind her, the world went dark.

"You should not have come, Emmie."

"Oh." She paused, leaving the dialogue sitting on the black screen. It wasn't the first time she'd seen a game use her own data against her, but she couldn't help a shiver. "I guess it must have mined my username from my computer," she commented for her viewers. "Almost clever."

She peeked at the chat.

"An Easter egg?" someone asked. "It didn't do that for other streamers, did it?"

"I thought the character's name was Miles."

"Spooky."

A frown tugged at her lips, but she didn't let it form. An Easter egg, indeed. If she was the first to encounter this apparent secret, at least it might gain the video a few more views.

She clicked away from the dialogue and the in-game Emmie pulled out a gray rectangle that was supposed to be a cell phone, turning on its flashlight. Dim details took form: the squarish shapes of a table and chairs, a grandfather clock with a swinging pendulum, a staircase, the closed door behind her. She turned her character around to check it; sure enough, it was locked.

"Shit," her character complained. Emmie commented about how her favorite curse seemed a little out of place in such an old-fashioned game. *"I'm trapped. I need to get both my sister and myself out of here before my phone's batteries run out."*

A battery counter, starting at 98%, faded in at the corner of the screen.

"You won't escape," the red text reappeared. *"We remain in the dark. Soon, so will you. You'll get what you deserve."*

She froze.

"You'll get what you deserve," EmmShadow had written on the back of the photograph.

A sour taste welled up in her mouth. Coincidence though the dialogue was, perhaps a horror game hadn't been the best choice for her first stream since the incident. She took a sip from her water bottle to pretend her pause had been on purpose.

She found the chat in the corner of her eyes:

"She's so pale already—nothing scary has even happened yet!"

"She's a good actor; I'll give her that."

"Why do you all like this girl? It's taking her forever to even get through the intro."

She suppressed a grumble and guided her character deeper into the house.

Lightning flashed, turning the game white.

For an instant, she saw it on the screen: a blank smile; bared, perfect teeth; narrowed blue eyes. The photograph.

A tiny scream escaped her, her chair jolting back on its wheels.

The game returned to normal while its buzzy thunder faded.

"OMG did you see her face?" fans wrote in the chat. "I think she seriously shat herself."

"That was barely even a jump scare!"

"One for the .gifs, for sure."

She took in a deep breath while her pounding heart slowed. She'd imagined that asshole's face; she must've. Man, her anxiety was getting to her. Lightning was the cheapest jump scare in the book.

"Guess I'm a bit out of practice," she chuckled for the camera. "Go easy on me, okay?"

***

The game was fairly straightforward. Through her character, Emmie searched the haunted manor for clues to her sister's disappearance and keys to unlock yet more pixelated rooms. All the while, a generic ghostly shape sometimes hunted her from behind, sticking to the dark. Simply shining her flashlight at it chased it off. Doing so, however, quickly drained the battery. There was an element of strategy to it: she had to stay alert for the ghost's presence but only face it when she truly needed to, lest she waste the game's only resource. Still, if she waited too long to stop the ghost or didn't catch it in time, it would strike from the shadows with a headphone-rattling screech and her batteries would plummet. Such jump scares weren't particularly scary, not after all the other horror games she'd played over the years. Still, Emmie hammed it up a bit for her viewers. She didn't entirely have to fake her discomfort, either. It wasn't the jump scares; it was the sensation of being chased—*stalked*—that stiffened her muscles beneath her charismatic veneer.

Yep. Going with a horror game today was definitely the wrong choice. I'm still more messed up than I thought.

She unlocked another in-game door. She'd reached the house's top story with about 30% of her battery left; if she was playing well, this would be one of the last rooms she had to explore. She entered—it was a bathroom. A mirror, a sink, a toilet, a window, a bathtub. A shudder took her by surprise. A shower curtain obscured the contents of the tub, but red stains rimmed its hem. "*It smells like blood,*" her character remarked on screen.

When Emmie sucked in a breath, a metallic tang hit her nose. A second surprised gasp only sharpened the smell: iron, salt, rot. Gooseflesh painted her skin. *Impossible.*

She was imagining things again; she had to be. Hair rose on the back of her neck, but she ordered herself to keep her eyes on the game. The whole point of this Let's Play was to show that she was still a top-tier ZTuber, that she was okay, so she needed to act the part.

After I finish this up I'll crack open a bottle of wine in bed, she promised herself.

She tried not to breathe through her nose as she went about solving the bathroom's puzzles. Shining her phone in the mirror made a hidden panel light up in the reflection. She moved her character toward it.

Drip, drip, drip.

The hair rose on her arms. The noise had to be coming from inside the game. The shower curtain fluttered with each drip. So why did it sound like it was coming from behind *her*?

Keep your eyes on the game, Emmie.

Drip.

The salty stench grew stronger.

She paused the game and took off her headphones.

"Emmie?" the chat asked over and over, so many different viewers typing the same questions.

"Why's she just staring like that?"

"I think she's actually freaked out!"

"You okay, Emmie?"

"She's got to be faking it!"

Drip.

Emmie looked at the camera and tried to smile. "Hold on for a minute, everyone. I'm picking up some noise IRL, and I don't want it interfering with the recording." She flicked off the webcam, then switched on the room lights.

Drip.

The noise couldn't be coming from the game, not with it paused.

Drip.

She swiveled around in her chair.

A drop of fluid fell from the ceiling. Another followed, joining the puddle on the floor.

Her heart squeezed in on itself.

Light reflected red off of the pool—red like blood.

She shut her eyes with a stifled cry. Her head swam, making her ears ring to the beat of her pounding heart. If she hadn't been sitting, she would've fallen.

I'm imagining things.

Even with her eyes closed, that sour tang spilled into her with every shaky breath.

Inside the game or out, I'm still just imagining things.

The stench didn't fade, coating the inside of her throat when she tried to breathe through her mouth. Her stomach twisted into a knot.

Maybe I'm not imagining things. Maybe it's not blood. Maybe there's another explanation.

She opened her eyes.

Another drop hit the floor and sent out red ripples.

Rust. That's what it had to be. The plumbing in her apartment was old, after all. A pipe must have burst and let out rusty water. That explained the iron smell, too. The leak had finally melted a hole in her ceiling and breached her studio.

Emmie let out a long breath.

She'd have to call a plumber after her video was over.

After taking a few minutes to fetch towels to wipe up the grim pool and temporarily plug the gap in the ceiling, she plopped back down in her chair and straightened her sweaty bangs before turning on the webcam. "Thank you all for your patience," she smiled. "I ran into some poorly-timed technical difficulties."

Her character wasn't where she had left it.

She blinked. The in-game Emmie stood in front of the sink. A towel that hadn't been there before jutted out of the faucet. She tapped the ENTER key to investigate. "*I stopped the leak,*" the character's dialogue said.

Drip.

A shiver touched her spine. The noise still sounded like it came from behind her, but... She didn't let herself turn around. She gave the ENTER key another click. "*I stopped the faucet from leaking,*" the character clarified. "*But it sounds like there's another leak coming from somewhere else.*"

"What the hell?" she couldn't stop herself from mouthing. "I didn't—Did I miss something?" she asked the chat.

"What do you mean, Emm?"

"Why's she look so confused?"

"She did zone out there for a few minutes. Bet she smoked a little too much THC before the stream."

"When I was gone, I mean," she clarified, trying not to let the tension in her muscles reach her voice. "Did I miss a scene?"

"Gone?" the chat echoed.

"You didn't go anywhere!"

"What's she up to now?"

"If you're trying to creep me out, it won't work!"

She shook her head at the camera. That—It didn't make sense. She'd paused the game, announced her break, turned off her camera, and fixed the leak in her studio. How could her viewers not have noticed? How could the game have kept playing? Why had the in-game Emmie fixed her leak in a way that seemed so much like...

She swiveled back around in her chair.

There was no hole in the ceiling, no towel to plug it, no rusty stain on the floor.

She had to be imagining things more than she'd thought possible. It must have been inside the game that she'd found a leak, fetched a towel, plugged it.

I'm losing it. Her pulse buzzed in her head and blurred the edges of her vision. She closed her eyes and counted to four, taking slow breaths until she could almost laugh. *A gamer who can't tell the difference between fantasy and reality. I'm turning into a damn cliché.*

She turned back to We Remain. A part of her pined to make an excuse and end the stream—after watching her zone out, her fans would likely believe her if she said she wasn't feeling well— but the other, more stubborn part pressed forward. Her willpower had gotten her this far, after all—had helped her make a living off something as silly as smiling and playing games. Now, it was personal.

Drip.

Steeling herself, she moved to the one place in the bathroom she hadn't explored: the tub. Her character flung the curtain away when she hit ENTER.

The sound that spilled out of her mouth wasn't a scream but a whimper.

A figure hung from the shower rod. Blood dripped from its lifeless toes into the crimson bath. Each drop was only a square pixel, and the dead man was only a stick figure, but the imaginary scent of death stung her nostrils.

"Shit," she hissed under her breath.

She tried not to think about the stalker who'd hung himself—or the way the temperature seemed to drop in her studio—as she completed the puzzle by taking a suicide note from the fictional corpse's pocket.

***

Only a 7% charge remained on her battery when Emmie guided her character into the manor's backyard. The note had ushered her there with a cryptic code, and there wasn't much to investigate save for a single gnarled tree. The sight of it, its pixels jagged and stark brown against black, sent chills through where her fingertips touched her keyboard. She walked up to it and pressed ENTER.

New dialogue appeared in red: *"Rest in Peace, Marjorie Gable."*

"What?" she stuttered aloud.

Marjorie Gable. Her legal name. It'd been far too old-fashioned to use as the bedrock for an online career, so she'd hidden it behind the pseudonym that had become her daily moniker. As far as her fans knew, Emmie *was* her real name. Now there it was: Marjorie Gable, printed across the screen in bright red font for everyone to see. She didn't use it anywhere on her computer; how had the damn game dredged it up?

She fought to flush the shock from her face. So long as she played it cool, no one had to realize there was anything strange about that name. "Guess that must refer to the sister," she managed. "Shocker: we're too late to save her."

"Should've known she was already dead," the chat box agreed.

"Buried in the backyard. Classic. RIP."

"The scares in this game are great, but the story sucks. I could've told you there was no chance of finding her alive. Boring."

"Emmie sure looks horrified, though. She must've actually wanted to save her."

"Aww, she's such a good person."

Emmie suppressed a sigh of relief. She clicked passed the dialogue. Her character found a key hidden by the makeshift grave—her ticket through the locked front door.

This time, she expected the lightning when it struck. The game went all out with its retro cinematics, sending white streams of pixels through the tree and setting it ablaze with square orange sparks. She expected it, too, when the ghost who'd been haunting her throughout the game appeared behind her. She even expected it when the electric current spread through the specter and lit up its shape with an eerie white glow.

What she didn't expect was the dread that washed through her own body.

Run, an instinct howled.

In a final flash of lightning, she saw it again: EmmShadow's blank smile on the blank screen.

She let out a cry and smashed the SHIFT key, sending her character sprinting toward the front door. With the now invincible ghost only pixels behind her, her battery drained quickly. 6%...

Escape escape escape!

5%...

Her heartbeat thrummed to the beat of the chiptune chase theme.

4%...

I have to escape, before...

3%...

The edges of the screen smeared as the ghost neared her heels.

2%...

The front door's window glimmered in her flashlight. *Almost there!*

1%.

The screen plunged into darkness as the flashlight died.

Her computer shut off with a hum. Her spotlights went out. Her mic let out a squeal before its indicator light went black. Soon, she was in darkness, too, as if her own power had gone out with the character's cell. Chilled air dried the sweat on her cheeks. The ceiling dripped behind her. Her gasps sucked in the stench of blood.

"No..." she whimpered, shutting her eyes. *Not real, not real, not real.* Her tense fingers squeezed tight around her mouse.

But it wasn't her mouse. Her nails cut into cold flesh. The hand she was holding grabbed tight to hers.

When her gaze jolted open, just enough light came through the door to show her EmmShadow's face. Gray, bloated flesh drooped from the bone. It was those eyes she recognized: the color of ice. "Come with me," he said, echoing the back of his photo. "You'll get what you deserve."

Emmie's scream wasn't captured on camera.

***

The live stream went dead at 9 PM. Fans clung to the chat for almost an hour, some angry, some worried. Many suggested that it must have been a power surge, ironically-timed though it was. A few called the timing a sign of conspiracy—a ploy for attention. "She's just trying to scare you—after all, that's all she's good for," one viewer wrote.

At midnight, another live stream started on Emmie's ZTube channel. Many of her most devoted, and most obsessive subscribers, stayed up late to watch it.

Emmie's face greeted them. As usual, she smiled through her webcam, but the most worried fans noted the tearstains on her cheeks. "Hello, geeks and gamers," her voice shook as she spoke. "I'm sorry about my earlier stream. It was—Well, something went wrong. I hope I didn't frighten you too much." Her grin shifted into a more genuine shape even as her eyes glistened like glass. "I just—I know I said it before, but I wanted to say it again: thank you, really. Thank you to those of you who've supported me, who gave me the chance to be myself and do what I loved. Whenever you told me I helped you smile, you helped me smile, too. I love you."

Her face changed, the smile twisting into a frown that swallowed the rest of her features. Later, when people paused the recording, they would find one frame where her eyes turned pure black. "To the rest of you—all of you who treated me like a fantasy to claim—I'm not surrendering. I won't go with you. If you've watched my videos you should already know one thing: I play to win." Each word seethed with rage. "You'll get what you deserve."

The video ended.

By morning, hundreds of bodies were found hanging from rafters and shower rods and balconies. The victims were from all over the world. Some of them still had their computers open to Emmie's midnight video. The police would later find one commonality between each suicide: each victim had left abusive comments in Emmie's ZTube inbox.

Emmie's body was found that morning, too. She'd hung herself from the ceiling of her studio with computer cords. Her death was ruled a suicide despite her autopsy showing signs of a struggle. Her time of death was estimated at 9 PM.

No one could explain how she'd live-streamed her final video three hours later.

ZTube and other video services purged the suspicious recording, but it lived on as an urban legend in the stranger corners of the internet. Rarely, and seemingly at random, it would re-upload to her channel with a timestamp of 12 AM and a few intrepid viewers would watch it before the censors took it down.

Not all of those viewers saw the next sunrise.

* * *

Airstream
By Ron Ripley

When Father Karl Durst returned from fishing Sunday afternoon, the silver Airstream camper was parked in the back of the church parking lot, close to the former convent.

Karl stood near his Chevy Caprice and stared at the camper, wondering which one of his parishioners would have the audacity to park such a monstrosity in the church's lot. Finally, with his fishing gear becoming uncomfortably heavy in his hand, he shook his head and walked toward the back door of the rectory.

I'll worry about it tomorrow, he thought, stifling a yawn. *All I have is the meeting with the deacons and a chat with the principal at St. Christopher's elementary school.*

Karl opened the door and let himself into the mudroom. He stripped off his fishing boots and set his poles and tackle box down. Leaning forward, Karl opened the small transom above the door, making certain no fish odors would be trapped overnight. Mrs. Lemieux was unforgiving when it came to the stench of fish in an enclosed space.

Doesn't matter that it's mid-October, Karl sighed, *or that I'm technically in charge of the entire parish. She is my housekeeper, and she will take me to task.*

He chuckled at the thought and unbuttoned his flannel jacket, hanging it on a peg near the door. Humming to himself, Karl walked into the kitchen, opened the refrigerator, and found the bottle of Stella Artois beer that Mrs. Lemieux allocated him on Sundays. Beside the beer was a plate which, he knew after long years, would contain a roast beef sandwich with spicy mustard and a pair of thick-cut tomato slices.

You are a wonderful woman, Karl thought, taking both the beer and the sandwich out. He carried them to the small kitchen table, sat down, and picked up the Sunday paper. Karl scanned the sports section to see who, exactly, was playing on Monday Night Football, and what the point spread was. After that, Karl ate his meal and skimmed the world news and local news sections, putting them down after reading nothing but death and mayhem across the world.

Can't we simply move beyond all this now? he thought tiredly. It was a question Karl had been asking himself for fifty years, ever since deciding he wanted to be a priest at the age of ten. He was tired of violence, and he couldn't understand why anyone else continued to fight. Karl shook his head, stood up, and took care of his mess, wishing the world would do likewise.

When the morning came, Father Karl saw the Airstream was no longer present, and so he put the thought of the trailer out of his mind. The week passed slowly and without much fanfare. There were no funerals to perform, nor were there any couples to counsel pre-marriage vows. Baptisms weren't scheduled until the end of the month, and trouble at the women's prison prevented him from leading the prison ministry group up to Concord. He visited the sick at St. Joseph's Hospital and stopped in at Greenbriar Nursing Home to attend to several of his flock there.

The week was entirely as it should be, and as it had been for years. A comfortable routine which delighted Karl and gave him a sense of purpose in the world. He made plans to eat with a nephew in the beginning of November and to attend a small conference at the Diocese in Manchester at the end of November. Finally, when Sunday arrived again, Karl performed the mass and was quite pleased with himself regarding the way he dovetailed the homily and the gospel reading.

Sunday evening, shortly after a fine repast prepared by Mrs. Lemieux, Father Karl decided upon a stroll. He put on his walking shoes, selected a cane from his collection of them by the front door, and at the last minute decided to bring bottled water on the off chance he worked up a thirst.

Better to have and not need, than need and not have, he mused, remembering the old adage.

With his water in his pocket and his cane in his hand, Karl put on his tweed cap and left via the rear entrance. He didn't bother with locking it. While the house had been burglarized once before, Karl still didn't approve of locking the door. After the robbery, he had helped Mrs. Lemieux inventory the home, looking for items that were missing. Along with his small collection of classic films on DVD, the trio of Chromebooks used for students who were tutored in the rectory, and a jar of change by the back door, Karl and Mrs. Lemieux discovered something utterly depressing.

Most of the nonperishable food was gone. The canned goods and the crackers.

It wasn't the fact that the items had been taken, rather it was why they had been taken. On a shelf in the pantry, there had been a note. It was on the back of the water bill's envelope, and the message looked as though it had been hastily scrawled.

I'm sorry. We're hungry.

There were no promises of returning the goods ten-fold as Karl had read of in the past. It was a simple statement and a disturbingly powerful one at that. The note served as a painful reminder of the shame that accompanied poverty and hunger.

With this bitter memory always fresh in his mind, Karl gave the doorknob a final check to make certain it was unlocked, and he walked down the short flight of stairs onto the parking lot's asphalt.

A flash of silver caught his eye, and Karl turned, surprised to see the Airstream in the same place as the Sunday before. The last rays of the sun caused the polished metal to gleam. Karl shook his head, amazed at the audacity of the parishioner as well as the sheer beauty of the machine. The windows set within the metal were all curtained, and the Airstream looked as though it might have been driven off the lot only minutes before.

Yet as attractive as it is, Karl thought, walking toward the trailer, *this is not the place to park it. I'll need to get the plate number and find out who this belongs to.*

Among the many small items Karl carried at all times, his most prized possessions were a fountain pen given to him by an aunt who served with the Sisters of Mercy and a notebook. He constantly filled notebooks with information about parishioners and ideas for various Church functions. The pen was refilled on a regular basis. In the past, Karl had used mechanical pencils, but they were never firm enough for him.

He took out the pen and the notebook as he reached the trailer. Karl looked to see if there was any information on the front of the Airstream, or near the door. When he went around to the back, he found the plate and stopped, surprised.

The plate was from Vermont, and it bore the date *1947.* There was no sticker showing it was registered, nor did the plate state that the vehicle was a trailer. Karl shook his head. With a sigh, he wrote down the number. As he put pen and paper away, he thought, *Did they change the rules regarding antique vehicles and trailers?*

Karl thought they might have. Since he didn't follow anything in the antiquing world, he wasn't surprised he didn't know.

Well, it will be an interesting subject to research, he thought. *Though I might be lucky enough to catch them returning to pick up the Airstream later on this evening or early morning if they keep true to form.*

With those thoughts occupying his mind, Karl headed out for his walk. He followed the long stretch of Ashland Street near his church, then turned into a back gate of Edgewood Cemetery. The paths were long and narrow, barely wide enough for a single car to pass through. Brightly colored leaves were scattered along the paths, and the wind picked them up and threw them where it would.

Karl inhaled deeply and enjoyed the coolness of the evening as the sun set beyond the western horizon. He paused and enjoyed the view, loving the entire experience.

I have a good life, he thought. *For that, I am thankful.*

Smiling, he took up his walk again and walked a long, circuitous route to the rectory.

As he approached the back of the convent, his eyes searched out the silver Airstream, but the trailer was gone. Karl reached the parking lot and stopped, shaking his head. Years ago, when he had first finished seminary and been ordained, he had briefly traveled with several other priests and laypeople. They did on the road missionary work in the forgotten parts of America, and they did it by traveling with a large pickup truck and a trailer. While the trailer they lived in and witnessed from wasn't the same size as the Airstream, it had still taken a significant amount of time for them to get the trailer connected properly to the truck.

I haven't been gone that long, he thought, frowning. Karl looked around, trying to spot the Airstream on the road further down towards Main Street.

He saw nothing except a small, dark blue sedan turning onto a side street.

Shaking his head, Karl went inside and poured himself a glass of cold water. He drank it slowly as he took off his coat and hat, returned his water bottle to the refrigerator, and then took out a packet of pre-packaged peanut butter crackers. The cellophane crinkled and complained as he opened it, and Karl popped an entire cracker into his mouth as he sat down at the table.

He glanced at his notebook and then flipped it open.

The numbers he had written down stood out, the black ink strong against the pure white background of the paper. Karl tapped an index finger on the number, wondering why the plate was unregistered.

It can't even pass as an antique plate, Karl thought. *It simply isn't right. Someone has to notice when it's being driven on a main road.*

Frustrated, and not positive as to why he was, Karl ate the remaining crackers and washed them down with the last of his water. The presence and then absence of the trailer, not once, but twice, irritated him in a way he couldn't explain.

It was though something was gnawing at the back of his neck. A fearful understanding of something which shouldn't be, but was nonetheless.

Karl left the kitchen, walked into the den, and stood there for a moment. He stared at his television, wondering if he should turn it on and see what game was being played. His newest book, an excellent collection of mysteries from authors old and new, lay on the coffee table in front of his chair.

Yet neither the television nor the book held any allure for him.

He wanted to know what had happened to the Airstream.

I need to stretch my legs again, he thought. He returned to the mudroom, put on his hat and coat, forewent the cane, and left the rectory. Father Karl hurried down the steps and stopped.

The Airstream was in the lot by the convent again.

No, Karl thought, shaking his head. *I didn't hear a truck. There was no noise. Or, was there? Was I so distracted I didn't hear the vehicle return and drop off the Airstream?*

As he tried to process the information, the old sodium lamps on the telephone poles flickered into life and bathed the trailer in their odd, orange glow. The sun finished its descent and night settled on New England.

Movement in the trailer caught and held Father Karl's attention.

One of the curtains had been peeled back several inches, then dropped back into place. He could still see the dull swing of the fabric.

This is absurd, he thought. *If someone is in there, I need to know what's going on.*

Karl didn't want to throw the people off the grounds, especially if they were in need. But he needed to know who they were and why they were there. The Church offered assistance if assistance was needed.

Karl tilted his head back, took a long, deep, and calming breath. Satisfied, he approached the trailer and knocked on the door. The metal was cold beneath his hand, and he shivered as he stepped back. From where he stood, someone in either of the windows which flanked the door would be able to see him.

He made certain to open his coat and reveal his priest's collar.

Once more, the curtain moved, but this time, the curtains in both windows. Nothing happened.

As Karl prepared to knock again, he heard a soft click and a thump, then the door opened.

A pair of children stood in the doorway. They were dressed in clothes too small for them, and they were gaunt as if they hadn't eaten properly in weeks, if not longer. While the children were similar in their tight features and with their shaky, unkempt brown hair, Karl wasn't sure if they were siblings or close relatives.

Hunger, he saw, had made them appear joined regardless of their bloodlines.

Karl smiled and forced his empathy down. *Emotions are for after the facts have been gathered,* he told himself.

"Good evening," Karl greeted them. "My name is Father Karl. Are you all right, children?"

The boy looked to the girl, and she nodded.

"Yes, Father," the boy answered, his voice thin. "We're fine. Thank you."

Karl smiled. "Are your parents home?"

They shook their heads.

"Where are they?" Karl asked.

"Trying to find dinner," the boy began, but the girl reached out and touched her brother, silencing him. His mouth clamped shut, and he stared at Karl.

"Trying to find dinner," Karl repeated. "I have dinner at my house. You are more than welcome to eat with me. Do you have a phone so you could contact your parents?"

They shook their heads.

Karl frowned. Even the most destitute tended to have at least one phone. "Really? Are you sure you don't want to come in and eat?"

"We can't," the girl said. "Our parents would be angry with us."

"Well," Karl smiled, "I could always bring food to you. Would that work?"

Both children nodded, smiling broadly and revealing off-white teeth in need of a good cleaning.

"Excellent," Karl stated. "Now, might I know your names. I feel terrible, just nodding to you both."

"Of course, Father," the little girl smiled. "My name is Beth, and this is Herman."

"Do you like peanut butter and jelly sandwiches?" Karl asked.

Herman looked confused for a moment, but Beth smiled broadly. "We love that, Father!"

"Oh, very good!" Karl chuckled. "That is about the extent of my culinary capabilities. I'll be right back."

He left the children standing in the doorway to the Airstream, trying not to think about how thin they looked in their outdated and ragged clothes. Karl hated poverty. It reminded him of the privileged life he had led as a child. He had never known want or hunger. The fact that they existed pained him.

Again he forced back his empathy and went into the rectory. He made a pair of sandwiches, took out a gallon water jug, and found a bag of unopened potato chips. For a minute, he stood in the kitchen, then he smiled and went to his secret stash of chocolate bars. He hid the Hershey chocolate from Mrs. Lemieux. She complained he was getting fat, and while he was a little heavier around the mid-section, he wasn't going to stop eating chocolate.

It was his only vice.

With his pockets loaded with chocolate, Karl put everything but the gallon of water in a shopping bag. He found himself humming as he exited the rectory. The door to the Airstream was still open, and the children remained standing in the doorway.

What strange children, Karl thought. He had seen such behavior in the past, though only rarely, and that when he was on the road ministering. Children who were hungry, or who had been abused to the point where they no longer focused on anything other than survival.

The idea that these children, that Beth and Herman might be living in a hellish world of abuse and starvation, struck Karl like a fist. His stomach twisted, and he swallowed convulsively. Catching his breath, he smiled at the children and thought, *I should have brought my cell phone. Well, I'll have to get it later.*

"Here you are," Karl said, handing the water and the bag to the children. They took it, smiling broadly at him. Reaching into his pockets, he removed the candy and gave it to them as well. "There, that's for after you eat your sandwiches."

"Thank you, Father," the children replied in unison. Beth nodded to Herman, and the boy put the chocolate in the bag and then brought everything into the depths of the Airstream.

"Would you like to come and sit with us, Father?" Beth asked.

"I don't know that your parents would approve of that," Father Karl replied. "They don't exactly know me. I am, for all intents and purposes, a stranger."

"Yes," Beth agreed. "But you are a priest. This is why we parked our camper here. There is safety in the Church."

Karl smiled, his heart swelling with joy. "Yes, I agree completely."

"Come in then, Father," Beth repeated. "There is room at our table for you."

The girl stepped aside and bowed slightly.

What a curious child, Karl thought, entering the camper. It smelled of nutmeg and cinnamon, of dry air and incense. Everything was neat and orderly, each surface cleaned. Herman stood at a small kitchenette and stared at the sandwiches as if he knew what they were but didn't quite understand why he had them.

Is he disabled? Karl wondered. *My goodness, are they leaving this poor child in the care of his sister?*

"Plates, Herman," Beth spoke gently as she unfolded a table from the near wall. She walked to her brother and helped take down a pair of plates. In silence, she showed him how to place first the sandwiches, then the chips on the plates. Herman carried the plates to the table and sat down, staring at his sandwich.

Karl watched as Beth took down a trio of tall glasses and filled them with water. Somehow she managed to carry all three glasses to the table. She set one down in front of her brother, one for herself, and then across from them.

"Will you sit with us, Father?" Beth asked, gesturing to the seat opposite them.

"Of course," Karl smiled. "Thank you."

He shivered slightly at the chill in the Airstream, but still, he unbuttoned the top of his coat. Karl picked up his glass to take a sip of water and noticed the glass was decorated with figures. He twisted it slightly in the light and chuckled.

"Muppets," Karl explained to the children as they peered at

him with confused expressions. "These glasses were available at McDonald's a very, very long time ago."

"That would explain why our father has them," Beth said. She lifted her own glass and took a small sip.

When she set it down, Father Karl looked at her. It appeared as though she had only wet her lips with the water, not actually drinking any of it. Herman leaned over his plate, sniffed the food, and then wrinkled his nose. The boy spoke in a language Karl didn't understand, and Beth laughed.

"He has not seen this type of food for quite a while," Beth explained as Herman stood up and walked to the door. He closed and locked it.

Maybe it'll get warmer now, Karl hoped. "What have you been eating?"

"A little of this, a little of that," Beth stated as Herman went around the camper and made certain the curtains were all closed. "Whatever our parents can bring home. We often go into the woods to hunt larger prey."

Karl blinked, confused. "You hunt?"

Herman's nod was enthusiastic. "Yes! I love to hunt!"

"I like to fish," Karl chuckled. "I was never one for a gun."

"Neither are we," Beth said, smiling. "We never use a gun."

"You two aren't strong enough for bow hunting!" Karl exclaimed. "You're far too small to even draw the bow."

"No," she whispered, "we don't use weapons. We don't have to."

"Then what are you hunting with?" Karl asked.

The children grinned at him, and he felt foolish, as though he was missing some obvious clue. He wanted to snap at them, but when he focused on their faces, Karl saw their teeth.

The incisors and the canines were long. Far longer than anything he had seen in his life.

Were they that long before? he asked himself. *No. They*

couldn't have been. I would have noticed.

His gaze focused on their expressions, and then his heart skipped a beat, then another.

The children's eyes were blood red. Their smiles were wicked things, full of hate and hunger. As he watched, their fingernails elongated, sharpening into points while the siblings watched him.

"We hunt," Beth said. "We hunt whenever we can. It is a joy to feast on them, to feel the blood coursing over our mouths, still warm, still stinking of fear. Fear is the tang that we love. Fear of death and, for people, what might be coming after."

Herman's tongue darted out and licked his pale lips.

"We are hungry," Beth continued. "We are always hungry. Rarely does dinner stride up to our home and knock. We appreciate your kindness, Father. It is a pity we cannot eat what you brought us, but we can eat you."

"No," Father Karl said, shaking his head. "No, you cannot. This isn't real."

The children laughed and exchanged words again.

"Of course, it is real, Father," Beth stated, tsk-tsking as he stood up. "Where are you going?"

"Out," Karl replied, his voice shaking and his hands trembling. "I need to go out. There is something wrong with you children."

"We are hungry," Herman hissed.

"My brother is correct," Beth agreed. "We are hungry, and you have brought us food."

"You can eat it," Father Karl said, disliking the predatory way the children watched him. "Children, get out of the way so I may leave."

"No, Father," Beth whispered, "you are the food you brought. You are our meal. Would you let us starve?"

"Stop it!" Karl screamed, fear racing through him. His head pounded, and his heart thundered against his chest. Panting, desperate for air, he felt his body begin to quiver. "I want to be let out."

"I'm hungry," Herman grumbled. "I want to eat."

"A moment more," Beth replied. Then, focusing on Father Karl again, she said, "Come now, Father, won't you sit down. It will be easier for us to feed."

Father Karl bolted for the door. The Airstream shook as his feet struck the carpeted floor and he reached over Herman for the door handle as the boy ducked to one side. As his hand closed on the cold metal latch, Karl was struck in the back of the head. He let go of the handle, hit his forehead against the metal frame, and staggered back. He bumped into the table, did a half spin on one foot, and crashed face-first onto the floor.

A cold weight climbed onto his back as he struggled to get up, but fingers grasped his hair and slammed his nose into the carpet, breaking it. He howled and tried to get up, but his broken nose was driven into the floor again. Karl tried to move, felt a hand close around his neck and squeeze. Gasping for air, he heard Beth's voice come from behind him.

"Do you smell it, Herman?" she asked, her voice sweet. "Do you smell the fear?"

"Yes," the boy whispered.

"Now," Beth sighed, "it is time to eat."

Father Karl Durst had no strength to scream as the children bit down upon his flesh and fed.

* * *

The Figure in the Scene
By David Longhorn

Yes, I know. Official statement—get it all down on paper. Well, tape, anyway. So, first things first. I steal things.

Aren't you shocked to hear that? No? Well, I suppose you deal with criminals all day long. But I'm not like them, you know. I don't steal things for money, to fuel some terrible drug habit, or whatever. Good gracious, no! I'm a rich widow, a respectable English lady, and if I was in need of cash, I could just sell that big house I've been rattling around in since my husband died— downsizing, they call it. So, my point is, don't confuse me with the dregs of society.

Why do I steal? It's fun, that's why. I need a bit of excitement in my life. Do you understand that? You look like a very understanding young man. Not hard-faced like some of the police these days. That girl on the front desk, dear me. Good poker player, I'd imagine. Record? No criminal record, no. Unless you count my copy of 'Agadoo'. Ah, such a nice smile! I knew you were a nice young man. Cruel people never smile with their eyes, have you noticed that? It never gets above the lips.

Of course, time is precious, I'll stick to the point. But I think it is necessary to explain why I'm seeking your protection— though I doubt that you can provide it, not with that thing there. Couldn't we go to another interview room, one without...? No? Oh, very well. Perhaps it will be all right so long as you are here.

After Gerald died, I never felt the need for a permanent relationship, though I took my pleasure with younger men as I liked. A forty-something woman in decent condition with a lot of cash to throw around never wants for male attention. But I was careful not to let anyone get too close to my heart, or my savings. Gerald left me very well-provided for, so I traveled, but that grows dull after a while. Then I attempted to cultivate friendships, a social circle. But I found women my age to be bitter divorcees or, even worse, suspicious hausfraus afraid I would steal their dull, flabby hubbies. Imagine!

So there was no love, as such, and no friendship. Family? God, no. Gerald's lot hated me from the start. His grown-up children saw me as the tart who stole their poor, smitten Daddy away from their mother. Whereas, in fact, the tedious bitch had practically bored poor Gerald to death long before I arrived on the scene. And then the cancer got her anyway, so I don't...

I was Gerald's secretary, yes, as it happens. Well guessed. But as I was saying, living alone in that house made me go almost insane with boredom. So I started to collect knick-knacks. Nothing too fancy, just little pieces of china, the odd snuff box, a few small bronzes—things to brighten the place up. To make it feel more like my home, you understand? Because when Gerald was alive everything had to be just so, his books neatly shelved, his records properly indexed, and no ornaments to gather dust. Dear me, no. So I suppose I was trying to regain a sense of my own identity after all those years of—well, call it domestic partnership.

Could I have a glass of—thank you, that's most kind. No, water's fine, I've had enough coffee to float a battleship these last few days. No, not much sleep.

Where was I? Ah yes, knick-knacks. Of course, I could have spent my time online buying from auction houses and dealers around the world. But I preferred to get out of the house and travel around, seeking out antique shops, house clearances, that sort of thing. I soon developed quite a good eye for a bargain, if I say so myself. It didn't take me long to spot con artists and people who were simply asking ludicrous prices. I began to resent this sort of thing, take it personally. Here was I, trying to make a new start for myself in the prime of life, and all these smarmy buggers were trying to rip me off!

What? Oh, no, it wasn't a deliberate way of striking back at them. The first time it was pure accident.

I was in a typically twee little antique shop in—well, let's call it Bray-on-Lye, a Welsh border town with a huge influx of summer visitors. It was hot, I was tired, and I hadn't found a single damn piece that I could afford. I remember picking up a piece of netsuke, you know, a Japanese carved wooden thingummy? Then a few moments later I was out in the street, in search of refreshment. When I found a seat at a pavement cafe, I ordered tea and cake, and paid in cash. It was when I was putting my purse back into my bag that I saw the netsuke nestling there among the used hankies.

I froze. I honestly had no memory of taking the damn thing, but there it was. I must have turned white, and God knows what expression I had on my face. The girl at the till asked me if I was all right. I blurted out something about the heat and went to sit down. I peeked at the stolen goods again, then covered it with my purse. For a mad moment, I contemplated returning it but wondered what the owner of the antique shop would do. He might call the police, for all I knew. And what kind of defense is "I didn't realize I'd done it"? You read about these things, confused old ladies getting done for shoplifting. And this piece of netsuke was worth hundreds.

Ah, yes—you're a very perceptive young man. The truth is I didn't want to return it. Mixed in with my panic, my fear, was a wonderful sense of being alive. I looked around at passersby and they seemed suddenly more interesting, genuine individuals and not just a bunch of dull suburbanites on a break. When the girl put my tea and cake in front of me, the colors, textures, flavors all seemed brighter, stronger somehow. It was an astonishing moment, as if I had discovered some new legal high...

Well, not quite. Not legal. But definitely a high.

I took the netsuke home and, at first, hid it at the bottom of a drawer full of old bras and knickers. I half-expected the police to burst in at any moment. Ridiculous, I know. But I was terrified, and it was a very pleasant kind of terror! And, of course, I stopped going to antique shops, fairs, whatever. I was irrationally convinced that I would run into the shopkeeper and he would—I don't know—point at me and shout, Stop, thief! Something like that. Silly.

But then the fear began to fade. And with it, of course, the pleasure of being afraid went. I could still take a little satisfaction in getting away with it. I took the netsuke out of the knicker drawer and found it a place on the old bookshelves. One of my young men—I forget which, maybe Darren—admired it, asked about it. I was rather thrilled to say it was very rare, expensive. That was quite a night.

And then, after about three weeks, the itch came. I had to go again, try it again. And I did. It was surprisingly easy the second time. I just identified something small enough to slip into my bag—a silver vinaigrette, as it happens—and made a clean getaway. Security cameras? Of course not. I made a point of checking for those first, casing the joint as they call it. You'd be surprised how many of these antique-trade sharks skimp on basic security. Or perhaps you wouldn't?

There was only one occasion when I was nearly caught, and that was my own fault. I was by far the richest-looking person in the shop, which was in a somewhat run-down market town. Of course, the proprietor scented money and hovered around me like a fly on—well, you know. Just when I thought he had been distracted by someone else he came back and caught me about to slip a silver cigarette case into my clutch bag. Well, he knew what I was about, and I could see that he knew, and so on. But in that moment, there was a kind of telepathic exchange of views, I think. He wouldn't say anything if I just put it back, so I did, and buggered off pronto.

That close shave proved valuable. I changed my modus operandi—isn't that what you call it? My M.O. I was used to dressing quite stylishly since I bagged Gerald. Nothing cheap looking, of course. No labels on display, but I was always elegant, understated. Then it occurred to me that looking wealthy was a bad idea, and I would be better off if dealers mistook me for an eccentric old bat. So I started to let the grey grow out in my hair, took to wearing tatty jeans and shabby trainers. I went for an off-duty librarian look, complete with wire-rimmed glasses in place of my contacts.

It worked! Suddenly I was the poorest-looking person in the shop, and I could go on the hunt at least once a month, sometimes more. I began to plan my excursions with military precision, using the internet to identify concentrations of likely shops and always going at weekends or on holidays so I'd have crowds to hide in. And my collection of knick-knacks grew, until I became quite proud of it. Every item had its own story, simply handling one gave me a little frisson of pleasure. A dirty kind of pleasure, and that's the best kind, isn't it?

Well, of course you have to say that, I quite understand. And I am getting to the point, really! It began when I found an oval metal box that I assumed was a jewel case. I just swiped it quickly and left, without examining it. All I know is that it was worth a small fortune. But when I was on the train home and opened the box, I found—could I have some more water, please?

Thank you.

I found that it had a small mirror inside the lid. There was nothing else, it was just a container for the mirror. This baffled me for a bit, but when I got home a quick search revealed that what I had was a Claude glass. No, not many people have, but it was in vogue in the early eighteenth century. You would go up a hill, you see, and then stand with your back to the landscape, and look at it in the small mirror. The mirror is quite dark, so the landscape would resemble a painting by a French artist called Claude Lorraine.

I know, why not just look at the nice landscape? But in those days people found wild nature a bit disturbing, I suppose. So they needed it tamed. And framed. And made darker, less intense. Oh, and another thing I found. About the glass. Another name for it is black mirror.

Well, I was a little disappointed by the Claude glass, I don't mind saying. The dullness of it seemed to spoil the thrill of the chase, you know? But it was rare, and I found myself playing with it, holding it up with my back to the window, looking out over the garden. Pretending to be a Jane Austen character, I suppose. Something like that.

That was the first time I saw him.

In the black mirror I caught a glimpse of someone moving out of sight, sort of half-shambling, but quite quickly. I turned around quickly and went to the window, but there was nobody there. Then the gardener, this chap who works three days a week, turned up. He was walking normally, but I waved at him, smiled. It must have been him, I thought. It was only later that I worked it out. That the gardener had been coming from the opposite direction to the shambling figure. There was no away he could have moved so quickly from one side to the other. But if there had been someone else—you see? How could the gardener not have seen them?

I put the Claude glass on top of the old bookcase and tried to forget about it. But I couldn't. I kept wondering what kind of optical illusion could have created that weird reflection. It preyed on my mind. I suppose I began to be afraid that I was seeing things, and that my brain might be turning to mush. You hear about retired people going gaga, don't you? I had to convince myself that what I had seen was a trick of the light or something.

But at the same time, I was scared I might see it again.

One night, just before bed, I found myself taking the thing down and standing in the same place, back to the window. This time, of course, it was dark, so when I turned off the lights in the room the black mirror reflected nothing. Then, as my eyes adjusted, I could just see the outline of the path and hedges in the faint light from the town. The house is set well back from the road, but it's hardly rural. As I made out more detail, I began to understand why people used the mirrors. It was rather pleasant, seeing my garden framed in that dim oval.

Then he appeared again. He was sort of shambling along again, jerky, moving like—well, I won't use the term, it's not nice, so let's say a person with a disability. I thought for a moment that he was on crutches or sticks, but then I realized that his body was all bent askew, legs and arms with too many joints. No wonder he couldn't walk properly. But he was moving quite fast, despite that. And this time he wasn't dodging out of sight. He was coming up the lawn. Towards the window, in fact.

I think I dropped the Claude glass. I remember switching on the light and then standing with my back against the wall, staring at the window. Of course, with the light on all I could see was my own reflection, looking like the cover of a Mills and Boon—wide-eyed in my dressing gown, hair all over the place. Nothing happened, and after a couple of minutes, I went to pick up the glass. It had fallen face down, and I was careful to keep the mirror facing away from me. I closed it and put it back on the bookcase.

And when I did that, something odd happened. One of Gerald's books fell off the top of the case, and just missed my head. I could have sworn I had sold or donated all of his stuff, but here was quite an old book of poetry that I had somehow missed. The last thing I wanted was to be reminded of the past, so I grabbed it rather roughly. A page came loose and fluttered away, so suddenly I was chasing bits of poetry across the room.

Yes, I know, but this is part of it, I'm sure. When I got the page, I was just going to shove it back into the book, but then something caught my eye. It was the title of a poem: 'The Figure in the Scene'.

Well, yes, how could it not remind me of the bloody mirror? Sorry. What's it about? Oh, Thomas Hardy writing about his dead wife, I think. Gerald used to read that stuff aloud to me, trying to improve my mind. I put up with it but I didn't take much in. I think that was one of his favorites. All about the silly woman sitting upon a rock or something, and Hardy remembering her while looking at the same rock. Dreary old sod.

Yes, I'm getting there! The point is that I lay awake that night—alone, if it's any of your business, just tossing and turning. When I did drift off there, I had this terrible recurring nightmare where I was on the slopes at Zermatt and Gerald was just beside me. I was encouraging him to have a go, but he was being an old stick-in-the-mud as usual. God, it was so hard to get him to even leave the bloody house, let alone go skiing! Of course, I could have been more patient. But the verdict was clear enough, he was careless. Those slopes need to be better marked, everyone says so. And then there was the weather—

Anyway, in the dream I pushed Gerald down the hill, and he tumbled over and over until he reached the bottom. That should have been the end, of course, but I didn't wake up. No, what happened then was that Gerald started moving again, sort of jerking and trying to get up. It took a while, but eventually he did manage to stand and then started to make his way back up towards me. Walking that horrible, jerky way, his legs and arms all broken to bits. In the dream I'm frozen, just staring down as he climbs up, getting closer until I can see his head bobbing horribly, sort of dangling sideways on his snapped neck.

God.

I woke up exhausted the next morning and decided to get rid

of the Claude glass. I could hardly sell stolen goods online, so I decided to simply smash it. I found a hammer and smashed it, hitting the outside of the case without opening it. I heard the glass break. Then I wrapped it in an old plastic bag and chucked it in the bin.

You see my mistake? No? Oh well. It was only later that day that I realized what I had done. I was getting ready to go out with a new beau. First date, so, of course, I started my preparations early. I was titivating myself in my bedroom when I caught a glimpse of something moving in the mirror. At first, I thought it was a tree branch outside the window, but it was inside the room. It was a thin, dark brown limb reaching around the curtain. It looked like it had two elbows, and the fingers were all crooked.

I probably screamed. I definitely ran into the bathroom and locked the door. I put my back against it, the way they do in films. Then I saw myself in the mirror above the basin. He was standing right next to me, turning that head on its broken neck, leaning down to kiss me with those dry, black lips.

Next thing I remember is running out into the street, then somebody called you. I really need you to lock me up. I can't think of anywhere else I can live. I need to be in a cell, and I'd rather not go to the funny farm if I can help it. Because I'm not mad.

You see? Breaking the black mirror didn't stop him, it set him free. Now he can come through to me any time he wants. I thought at first he was trying to hurt me, or at least scare me. But now I wonder if he still loves me, in spite of everything. In a way, that would be worse.

Here? I don't know, he might be. I don't want to look. I don't want to look in your bloody two-way mirror!

**

The Detective Sergeant looked down at the shards of glass

still littering the floor of the interview room. It was a scandal, perhaps even a career-ender. Certainly, he had no chance of promotion in the immediate future, maybe never. Reviewing the tapes, both audio and video, had left no doubt what had happened. An officer in charge of questioning had failed to secure a mentally disturbed individual, the woman had killed herself, and the press already calling it a tragedy.

She moved so fast, though. As if she was being dragged...

One moment the woman had been shouting, her back to the mirror, as the Detective Sergeant tried to calm her down. He was just stepping around the table when she had turned, jerking around, off-balance, so that he feared she was having some kind of fit. But instead, she had hurled herself forward into the sheet of glass, going through headfirst. By the time he reached her she was lying like a broken doll, half out of the interview room, midriff secured by a spike of broken glass. She had been dead long before the paramedics arrived.

The video footage had shown all that. But the camera angle had been wrong, so that the officer had not been able to set his mind at rest on one point. As she had crashed into the mirror, he had thought he had glimpsed, just for a moment, a tall, thin figure clutching the woman to its wasted frame as if in a bizarre waltz. For an entity that moved like a damaged spider, it had been surprisingly fast. The face of the shadowy being had been impossible to make out in detail. But the officer felt sure he had seen a smile on its lips.

"Maybe old Gerald did still love her," he muttered. "But I wouldn't bet on it."

* * *

Volume 2

The Rain Runner
By Rowan Rook

Rocked in the cradle of the deep,

The song echoed in Trevor's mind as he sunk. With skin already numbed by the icy water, it felt like falling through the air. He had no better chance at swimming than flying. All his life, he'd tried his best. He got good grades, listened to his parents, liked studying new topics. The only thing he'd never been able to learn was how to swim. He knew he should try, but his body was as frozen on the inside as on the outside. All he could do was reach one small hand toward the last of the surface's light as the ocean's black swallowed him up.

I lay me down in peace to sleep;

The song grew louder in his head, surging into the silence inside his drowned ears. "Rocked in the Cradle of the Deep" by Emma Hart Willard, as clear as if his mother was there to sing it while they swayed in her rocking chair. He'd been far too young then to tell her it scared rather than soothed him. Sometimes he blamed the lullaby for the nightmares, and sometimes he blamed the nightmares for not learning to swim. Maybe this was just a nightmare, too. Maybe he hadn't fallen off the dock. After all, he was a good boy. He wouldn't have been reckless enough to run along the water... would he? He couldn't remember anymore. His thoughts blurred and sagged, as if the water was flooding even the inside of his mind.

Secure I rest upon the wave,

Pain swelled in his chest, his lungs screaming for air, and his freeze instinct turned to fight. His limbs flailed as if it was electricity washing over him instead of water. Bubbles, barely visible in the filtered specks of sunlight, left him behind as they fled for the surface.

His heart hammered against his burning chest.

Soon, there would be no more light, not ever. The black would swallow him whole. He'd never start 5th grade, never get to play the next *Pokémon* game, never get to grow up. He'd float, dead, to the bottom of the sea. Fish would nibble at his toes and fingers and eyes. Finally, the muck and seaweed would bury his bones. Consumed. Lost. Forgotten.

He screamed, the last of his air turning to bubbles and abandoning him.

For thou, O Lord! hast power to save.

Save me, he pleaded with everything as his vision turned as dark as the ocean. The last thing he saw was a distant splash from far above, sending down shivers of light like splinters of glass.

Save me...

***

"Shit." Trevor's hands shook as he tried the key again. The car shook, too, gurgling and sputtering like something out of his drowning dreams. It choked and left him sitting in silence on the side of the road. "Not now, not now, not now!" It took all of his restraint not to slam his fists into the steering wheel.

He couldn't be this unlucky. The forecasters being wrong about the storm reaching Las Vegas was bad enough. His car couldn't pick *now* to give out on him.

Trevor tried again, gritting his teeth.

The car didn't even grace him with a sound.

Dead.

He slumped in his seat, and after a swallow, dared a look out the windshield. The sky was gray, roiling with strands of sunlight interspersed with black, wet wisps. The rain would be there soon. It... was going to catch him. He rubbed his trembling hands together and tried not to cry. He hadn't let the rain actually reach him in years. He'd forgotten what it felt like to sense the needles on his skin, gasp for oxygen, hear the call. During dry summer days, he sometimes tried to convince himself that he was simply mad—that he'd made it all up. A delusion brought on by trauma, as his counselor insisted. But now, as the damp air sneaked in through his vents, an electricity raised the hairs on his neck.

He should've listened to his first instinct and left Las Vegas when even the possibility of rain appeared in the news. The forecasters had seemed so sure they'd stay dry, but the night before had been the first he'd dreamed of his near-drowning in a long time—always a bad omen.

The memory—the black, the cold, the lullaby—replayed in his body. He'd fallen off the dock during a cousin's beach birthday party and when his uncle had pulled him from the ocean, he'd already been unconscious. The first responders had declared him dead at the scene. His parents called the way he burst back to life, suddenly spitting out water and screams while they sobbed over his body, a miracle.

For a while, he'd considered it a miracle, too. But he'd never gotten his life back, not really. The first time he'd gone into the bathroom alone and washed his hands, the presence of water seemed to come with whispers and the touch of it on his skin submerged him in the sensation of drowning. A drop of it was enough to make his lungs ache for air they suddenly didn't have. At first, he and the doctors thought it was hallucinations—all in his head—but when his parents found him passed out in the shower, more water in his lungs than he could have swallowed and his memory of the last few minutes replaced by blank terror, they all began taking his new phobia a bit more seriously.

He stopped showering, cleaning himself with only rags and soap and washing his hands with sanitizer, avoiding running water or any body of it bigger than a toilet bowl. He even stopped drinking it, jealously guarding a supply of soft drinks and juice boxes. The rain, though... the rain was the worst. Each drop stung his skin, and the sight of it blurring the world through the windows squeezed the oxygen from his chest. Sometimes, he'd hear the voice, strangely familiar as it hummed that familiar song. For hours later, he'd cough up water he hadn't swallowed. His father left after the first storm, hissing something about demons after a drunken argument with his wife. Trevor and his mother packed their bags and moved to Las Vegas, the USA's driest city. Whenever the forecasters predicted rain, they left, traveling deeper into the desert or wherever else the weather maps promised they'd find clear skies. Even after cancer claimed his mother, Trevor continued to run from the rain.

He could never have a steady job. He could never have a girlfriend or a family. He could never live a normal life. Not when the weather report on any given night might send him fleeing for his life, or at the very least, his sanity.

This time, he hadn't left soon enough. He'd put too much trust in the forecast instead of his own honed instincts. He would've still made it if only his car hadn't—

The first drop of rain hit the windshield with a thunk.

Air gushed out of his lungs as if it had struck his chest like an arrow, instead.

Seconds passed as he stared at the unfamiliar sight, the water carving a trail down his window like a spider building a web.

"*I know thou wilt not slight my call,*" a voice whispered as if from beside him, rumbling like the ocean.

Adrenaline shot up his spine as he spun toward the passenger seat. Empty. A drop of water leaked through the roof and tapped the floor.

"For Thou dost mark the sparrow's fall," the song filled up the car.

Trevor shoved open the door and burst into the rain. He pulled up his hood and ran. Each drop that touched his skin smoldered like fire and left behind trails of vapor.

And calm and peaceful shall I sleep, his mind compulsively sang on.

His muscles moved like sludge as he fought for breath. Pressure swelled in his chest with each step. If he couldn't escape the rain, he needed to find shelter—somewhere that wouldn't leak, where he could close the blinds and close his eyes and pretend this was just another nightmare.

Rocked in the cradle of the deep.

***

"Are you okay?" The wide-eyed motel clerk hung back, bouncing on his heels as if torn between running to help or ducking behind his desk. "Sir?"

Trevor coughed another mouthful of water onto the carpet. He looked away from it quickly and tried to pull his voice through his aching throat. "I need a room," he managed.

"Umm," the clerk blinked, his own words coming out tight. "We won't have any ready for another few hours. It's too early. They haven't been cleaned out yet."

"It's fine," Trevor fought the urge to spit another bullet of water at the floor. When he swallowed, he tasted salt. "Just get me a room. My car broke down. I'll pay extra."

The clerk relented with a sigh, pushing up his glasses. "Take Room 4, then. It's $87 a night."

Trevor dared a glance back at the window as he fumbled with his wallet. Raindrops fogged the glass between the motel lobby's drab red curtains.

"*When in the dead of night I lie,*" the voice sang.

The world blurred at the edges.

"Sir?"

Trevor startled back into his skin to meet the pale-faced clerk. A room key sat on the desk in front of him. His fingers trembled as he took it and whatever pride he had left wilted when he forced a smile. "Will you walk me to it?"

The clerk only offered another blink. "It's right out front. You'll find it."

Dread at the thought of stepping back into the storm clenched in Trevor's stomach. "Can't you show me? Please?"

Sometimes, with someone to talk to, it was harder to hear the voice.

***

Trevor sat alone on his motel bed while the rain beat against the roof. What a strange, unpleasant sound—countless tiny drumbeats. It was hard for him to believe most people ignored the rain or even found it pleasant. He heaved into the sleeve of his shirt, leaving a wet stain behind.

At least getting the water off of him seemed to help. Upon arriving in the small hotel room—only a living area barely big enough for a bed and a thin bathroom by the door—he'd checked all the windows to ensure they were sealed and closed all the curtains. The tap had been dripping, but it'd stopped after he twisted the handles tight. He'd wrapped his damp coat in a towel and left it on the bathroom floor. He'd forgotten to grab the suitcase of clothes from his car, but, thankfully, his jacket had done its job and left his clothes mostly dry. So long as he could drown out the voice, then perhaps he could wait out the rain, after all. He only wished he'd succeeded into goading the clerk into staying for a while longer, but the man had seemed to sense Trevor's own tension and had been all too eager to return to the safety of his desk, as if some part of him sensed that the rain wasn't safe, at all.

"And gaze upon the trackless sky."

Trevor stiffened, his eyes pulled to the window's closed curtains.

"The star-bespangled heavenly scroll."

"Ignore it," he told himself aloud, even as the anxious part of his mind—the part that wanted to stop running and get *it* over with, whatever it was—itched to follow along with the song.

"The boundless waters as they roll—"

Trevor switched on the TV. He squirmed while he sat through a few stories about school levies and local sports, barely able to hear the news anchors over the pounding in his rasping chest. He mouthed a silent prayer as what he'd been waiting for arrived: the weather report.

"Expect scattered showers through the night," the forecaster said. "By the morning commute, the worst of the storm should have passed and we'll be seeing temporary sunbreaks. We're in for a soggy couple of days, but this is the first real weather event of the season, so at least our gardens will—"

The volume cut off as the lights flickered.

"I feel thy wondrous power to save," filled in the hush.

Gooseflesh prickled through Trevor's skin.

"Don't go out," he pleaded with the power.

The electricity whined with another surge. This time, the world stayed black. Black like the bottom of the sea.

A drop of water—from where, he couldn't say—hit Trevor's flushed cheeks. Chills spread out like cracks in his face. It left a cold trail behind as it traveled down and dripped from his chin like a tear.

His tongue mouthed the next line on its own, "From perils of the stormy wave."

Pipes shuddered and squealed in the walls. Raindrops pelted the windows until their beats merged into a single, ceaseless roar. The sound of gushing water splashing onto porcelain echoed from the bathroom—the tub.

Trevor squeezed his eyes shut and bit down on his tongue to keep the lyrics from coming. This wasn't possible. A storm couldn't, wouldn't, come pouring out through the plumbing, not like this. It was all too intentional, too molded to his own fears. It had to be a nightmare, after all.

But the burning ache in his lungs—real pain—meant that it wasn't.

He counted backward from four over and over again in his head, trying to sync his brain to the beat of the numbers rather than the rumble of rain—so much like the underwater rumble of the sea—and trying to convince himself he could still breathe. Liquid rattled in his chest with each gasp at the salty air.

"Rocked in the cradle of the deep, I calmly rest and soundly sleep."

Cold water touched his toes. His eyes jerked open and he tried to shout, spitting up sour coughs. Impossible. He didn't know how long he'd counted in his head, but it couldn't have been long enough for water to pour out from the bathroom. It seeped in from beneath the front door, too, and leaks from the ceiling poured in fresh, rippling rivulets. The floor was flooded. Its slick surface glistened in what dim light still pushed through the curtains.

Trevor's thudding heart nearly hammered away his

consciousness. He wobbled on the bed, the adrenaline in his system screaming over fight or flight.

"*Stay*," said the voice.

Shivers electrified Trevor's spine. Somehow, the voice was so much worse without the lyrics. It almost sounded like his own, deeper and wetter.

"*Come to sleep, now.*"

Sleep. If only it was as easy as falling asleep. If only drowning didn't hurt. Otherwise, the black almost would be like a blanket, the sway of the waves like a cradle. He could collapse back on the pillow and simply float away.

"*Don't keep running; rest.*"

Don't keep running...

As if he had the option to run, now. His bed had become an island, and soon, it'd be nothing inside the rising flood. His eyes fell on the front door, its damp knob shimmering like the ripples. He couldn't escape, not without passing through the water.

He leaned over as a cough rocked through him, water pouring up from his lungs and splashing into the rest of the tide. The surface below him looked as dark as the ocean at night. But it couldn't be as endless. Even if this wasn't quite reality—it couldn't be—it hadn't yet reached the top of the bed. He... could still walk through it. He wouldn't have to swim, not yet, not if he hurried.

His insides recoiled at the thought of touching water, of letting it suck at his legs and numb his skin. The voice was right: he couldn't keep running. His only other option was to surrender.

Save me, a drowning boy had once pleaded at the Universe.

And the Universe had answered.

"And such the trust that still were mine." Trevor swung his legs into the water. Ice splashed up and smoldered at his cheeks. Vertigo pulsed at the back of his head. He hadn't felt the soft, strange touch of liquid in so long. It seemed to stick to him, spreading inside through the numb tingles that seeped through his skin and into his bones, like it would never quite let him go. "Though stormy winds swept o'er the brine," he sang, letting his own voice echo louder than the one behind him. The flood sloshed with each step, retreating before surging back toward him like a tide. The lyrics rattled while pressure squeezed tighter around his chest, "Or though the tempest's fiery breath."

"*Stay!*" the command made the water vibrate around his ankles. "*Sleep.*"

He didn't. "Roused me from sleep to wreck and death." He kept moving, always focusing on the next words instead of the pain and his pounding heart, "In ocean cave, still safe with Thee The germ of immortality!"

"*You were never supposed to escape!*" the false sea screamed.

But Trevor's fingers found the doorknob and turned it.

Light poured into the room like liquid itself, the sickly gold of streetlamps. Trevor's lungs cleared with a final, gushing cough, and the tarry night air rushed inside them. Rain tapped the sidewalk in front of the porch's awning in a slow, perfectly normal rhythm. Faint electricity glowed from behind the closed-curtained windows of several other motel rooms, also perfectly normal, as if the dark had been confined to his. For a while, he simply breathed, each gasp heavy with petrichor. When he finally dared to look back, the motel room was dry, save for a few drops of water squeezing through a leak in the ceiling. He almost laughed.

***

The sun had already risen when the rain stopped. Trevor had spent the rest of the night perched on the porch, waiting out the storm in a place where he hadn't felt trapped. The voice had whispered to him once or twice, but he refused to run or hide, simply watching the drops fall. Nonetheless, he barely held back a shout of joy when blue sky cut through the clouds.

He ventured back into his room only once to snatch his wallet from the bedside table. Last night's forecaster had said the sunbreaks would be temporary. He needed to keep moving, farther away from the storm. One night of bravery had been quite enough for now. Perhaps he could catch a bus—perhaps even a bus to the airport. California was supposed to be sunny and dry this time of year. Maybe he'd even whisk himself away to Chile's Atacama Desert and never look back.

Water splashed up under his boot as he stepped off the porch. He looked down.

His own face stared up at him—a reflection painted in the puddle by the sunrise. But it wasn't right, wasn't really his reflection at all. Its skin was gray and bloated, his shape smeared like an insect's after smacking into a windshield. Its eyes were blank, lifeless, *drowned.* Because he hadn't stepped outside after a rainstorm in so long, had avoided every pool or lake or pond, he hadn't seen himself reflected in water in years. ...How long had it looked like this?

"*You weren't supposed to escape,*" his reflection repeated. "*You weren't supposed to be saved. The water wants you back.*"

His reflection's cold, wet hands wrapped around his ankle.

Before he could scream, Trevor was falling. Water consumed him with a splash. The liquid stirred and bubbled up around him as he flailed, but never let go, numbing him, pouring inside through his ears and nose and startled, gaping mouth. All he could do was reach one hand—bigger now, but just as helpless—toward the last of the surface's light as the abyss' black swallowed him up.

Save me, he pleaded with everything as his vision turned as dark as the nightmare he'd never really escaped.

This time, no one would ever find him. He'd float to the bottom, if this abyss even had one, his bones never again touching

the light. Consumed. Lost. Forgotten.
　　His lungs screamed for air before they burst.

And calm and peaceful shall I sleep.
Rocked in the cradle of the deep.

* * *

The Funeral of Sam Butler
By Ron Ripley

"You ready for this?" Billy asked.

Shane finished his cigarette, rubbed the butt out and field-stripped it before he answered. "'Course not."

He put the remnants of the cigarette in his suitcoat's pocket.

The two of them walked away from Billy's pickup, and each adjusted their clothes. Shane glanced at the sky, eyeing the dark clouds creeping in from the west. A cool breeze raced low along the cemetery, rustling the leaves of the trees along the outskirts of the gathered plots. Shane's hands itched to find a cigarette, and he forced them to be still.

In silence, the two men walked along the grass path, through narrow aisles between generations of families buried between granite and marble borders. Ahead of them, the funeral party stood. A trio of old men in Marine Corps uniforms sat in metal folding chairs, and the pastor stood at the head of the grave. On top of the platform which would lower it into the ground was a sleek, black coffin, the end visible beneath a large American flag. Off to one side stood the honor guard of Marines, their rifles and themselves at parade rest. The Marines responsible for the flag stood near the pastor, conversing with him in low tones.

Shane took all this in as he and Billy walked up to the graveside. There was a pair of empty chairs beside the old Marines, and all three of the men looked up at Shane and Billy. Shane eyed the ribbons and medals on the men's chests, registering battle stars for Korea and Vietnam, purple hearts and bronze stars, silver stars.

All three men wore Navy Crosses.

The men, Shane saw, had nearly identical features. There were slight differences in chins and lips, a nose a hair larger, eyes ranging from hazel to blue. Scars on the face of one, fingers missing on the hand of another. They were salty, as the Marines liked to refer to their own who had seen and done things others could only dream of.

The old men looked at Shane and Billy, eyes assessing and judging.

"Billy Ferman," Billy said, extending his hand.

The old man in the center shook it, nodded, and said, "I'm John Butler. These are my brothers, James and Geoffrey."

"Shane Ryan," Shane said, and the five men shook hands all around.

"My nephew, Sam, he spoke about you a lot," James said as Shane sat down beside him.

"Anything good?" Shane asked.

James shook his head.

"Didn't think so," Shane said.

Billy leaned forward, looked at the Butler brothers, and asked bluntly, "Who found him, and how did he do it?"

The question had been bothering Shane and Billy, and it was one they had discussed at length on their drive from Massachusetts to Pennsylvania.

"I did," John answered.

"He used a .45," Geoffrey added.

Billy swore under his breath, and all the men nodded.

"Did he leave a note?" Shane asked.

James looked him in the eye and said, "He did. But my nephew blew his brains out over it. Kind of made it hard to read. What little I saw mentioned Afghanistan. Know about it?"

Shane nodded as Billy looked down at the grave. "He killed a couple of kids and their moms."

None of the older men flinched at the statement.

"Did he have a reason?" James asked.

"Yup," Shane answered. "Moms, they went for AKs. When

they were put down, the kids went for them."

"How long did he carry that?" John asked.

"Ten years," Billy said softly. "Tried to talk to him about it. Tried to get him to talk to anybody about it."

"No, no reaching him," Geoffrey said. "His father was the same way."

"Funny thing," John said, "his father used the same damned pistol to kill himself."

Silence settled over them then, and the pastor took the opportunity to start the funeral service.

Shane had buried a great many friends, and he had put a few in the ground himself. The sound of taps pulled at him, and the rattle of the rifles reminded him of other burials.

When all was said and done, when the Marines had folded the flag and presented it to James, the eldest of the Butler brothers, the old men invited Shane and Billy back to the nursing home for a bit of reminiscing. But it was a perfunctory gesture, and both Shane and Billy recognized it as such. They politely refused and walked with the old men back to the van, which would bring them back to their home.

Soon, they were alone in the cemetery with the gravediggers filling in Sam's grave.

Shane lit a cigarette and looked out over the small cemetery, and movement caught his attention. Far in the left corner, hardly visible in the shadows, was a middle-aged woman. She was plump, clad in clothes at least fifty years old, and frightened. As Shane watched, she ducked behind a mausoleum.

Something's wrong, he thought. He took a long pull off his cigarette. After a moment, he turned to Billy, "Hey, I think I'm going to stay here for a bit."

Billy looked at him in surprise. "You serious?"

"Yeah," Shane nodded. "I've got some friends in the area. I think I'll give them a call, see what they're up to."

Billy eyed him carefully. "You sure about this, Gunny?"

Shane grinned. "Billy, I'm never sure about anything. How do you think we got out alive?"

"We got out alive because you were the meanest man in the Marines Corps, Gunny," Billy said evenly. He extended his hand and Shane shook it. "Hey, I know people say this all the time, but seriously, let's not wait until the next funeral to get together. I'm an hour away in Boston."

"I know you are," Shane said, no longer joking. "We'll get together. I don't do much anymore."

"Did you do much, to begin with?" Billy asked, dodging Shane's punch easily. "Heh, all right, Gunny. I'll see you soon. Don't kill anybody."

"No promises," Shane waved as Billy went to his pickup, climbed in, and left.

Shane stood still for a moment, then he walked out of the cemetery to the main road. He paused, then turned left, heading in the direction of a small plaza they had passed on their way in. A few vehicles passed him, and after ten minutes, Shane walked into the plaza, his feet leading him to a store called, *Fine Wine and Good Spirits.* The door chimed as he entered, and he stopped to get his bearings.

A young man smiled at him from behind a cash register and asked, "Hello! Are you looking for anything in particular?"

Less joy, Shane wanted to say. Instead, he smiled and replied, "Whiskey."

"What type?" the young man asked.

"Whatever type is cheap and can get me drunk," Shane said.

The young man chuckled, realized Shane was serious and cleared his throat uncomfortably. "Um, the back wall, sir, is where you'll find our selection of fine whiskeys."

"Wet and cheap," Shane said, smiling. "That's all I need out of it."

Leaving the young man to ponder his statement, Shane walked to where the employee had indicated. Squatting down, Shane saw a fifth of Steinbeck's Wild Irish Whiskey for ten dollars, and he grinned.

He carried two of them to the register and refrained from chuckling at the sight of the young man's wide eyes. The employee rang them up, placed them in a bag, and said, "Well, I hope these will last you."

"Me too," Shane said. "I don't want to have to come back before you close tonight."

He waved goodbye to the open-mouthed young man and left the store. Shane went next to a small convenience store, bought some premade sandwiches and water, tossed in a few bags of licorice, and then stopped. Grinning to himself, he picked up two containers of Morton's table salt. Carrying everything to the counter, he made small talk with the man working and left the store whistling. It was only in the last store, a general goods establishment, that Shane became disgruntled.

The teenage girl and boy working behind the desk stared at him, reminding him of his scars and his alopecia. He wondered how the complete lack of hair and mangled scalp appeared to them, and he wanted to whisper, *Boo*, just to see how they would react.

Like idiots, I suppose, Shane thought. He placed all his previous purchases in a cart, paused in front of the desk and grinned at them, making sure they could see his missing teeth. "Say, do you have a family planning section in here?"

The girl's eyes widened, and then she blushed furiously. Her companion looked at Shane, confused. She shook her head while the boy asked, "What?"

"Something your parents should have used," Shane said politely. "Too bad. Anyway, poncho and a backpack?"

Both the teens pointed to the back wall. Shane nodded his

thanks, winked at the girl as leeringly as possible, then turned and continued his shopping.

By the time he was finished, Shane was outfitted for a night in the cemetery, which he suspected he was going to have. He left the teens at the store in a decidedly flustered state, and he felt good about it. His food and alcohol were safely put away in his pack, as were the extra clothes and the poncho he had purchased. Shane had even found a decent blanket.

When he returned to the cemetery, the workers were gone, a fresh mound of dirt on Sam's unmarked grave. Shane paused in front of it, lit a cigarette and said, "I'm sorry you went out like this, Sam. I really am. Hope you're okay now."

With that said, he walked to the far corner where he had seen the dead woman. Shane caught a glimpse of her out of the corner of his eye, and he whistled cheerfully as he set up his camp close to where she was. When he finished opening his whiskey and eating a sandwich, he stretched out, put his hands behind his head, and looked up at the sky. He felt the temperature of the air change gradually, sinking lower and lower until he could see the woman standing next to him.

In a soft, gentle voice, Shane said, "I know you're there. I can see you."

The woman covered her mouth to keep a gasp from being heard, but she didn't move.

Carefully, Shane turned his head towards her, and he saw her eyes widen.

"I'm going to sit up now," Shane said, "I just want to make sure you're okay."

She took a nervous step back, but she didn't run away.

Shane sat up cautiously, making certain not to move too fast.

"My name is Shane," he said. "What's yours?"

"Joan," she whispered, lowering her hand. "I'm Joan Carr."

"Hi, Joan," Shane said. "It's nice to meet you."

"How can you see me?" she asked, still whispering.

"It's just something I can do," Shane answered.

"You're not like her, are you?" Joan asked, taking another step back.

"Like who?" Shane asked.

"The one who put me here," Joan said bitterly. "I was happy!"

"Who put you here, Joan?" Shane asked, feeling his anger rise. "Did someone kill you?"

She shook her head. "I died from a fever. Then, I woke up, I was still in my house. Still with my family. My son, he still lives in the house, with his children. I was able to see my grandchildren every day!"

"What happened, Joan?" Shane asked. "Can you tell me?"

She nodded. "A woman came into the house, with a ghost, and they chased me out. She found my necklace and knew I was attached to it. Then, she brought it here and buried it with my grave. I can't go back!"

Shane brought his temper under control and said, "I can dig the necklace up. I'll bring you back to your house."

She shook her head, fearfully. "No," she whispered. "You can't."

"Why not?" Shane asked.

"Because she buried him with me," Joan sobbed, pointing.

Shane jerked his head around and swore.

The ghost of a giant man towered above Shane as he scrambled to his feet. Before he could get fully clear of the dead man, Shane was thrown backward, his head striking the side of the stone mausoleum.

***

He coughed, spat blood, and tried to see. The darkness around him sought to induce panic, but Shane pushed it aside as he struggled to gather his thoughts. His heart pounded out a slow, steady, almost nauseating rhythm as he pushed himself onto his hands and knees. It was then he felt cold stone beneath his hands.

Where the hell am I? he wondered, his head aching.

Before he could answer his own question, he heard a woman's voice.

"What do you mean he saw you?" she demanded.

Not Joan, Shane thought, his thoughts painfully slow. He dragged himself toward the sound, finding a wall with his hands and creeping along it. His eyes pulsed to the beat of his heart, and he had difficulty making out exactly what was said.

"Exactly what I said," a deep, bitter voice responded. "He saw me. Wasn't gunna but he did. Threw 'm into the crypt."

"It's a mausoleum," the woman said angrily. "Wait. Did you say he's in the mausoleum? Right now?"

"Yup," the dead man responded.

"Is he dead?" she asked carefully.

"No, Janet, he ain't dead," the ghost answered. "Youse is always sayin' I can't kill nobody without permission."

"You really are dumber than a box of bricks, Henry," Janet spat. "Get in there and finish him off."

"Can't we close the door and leave 'm?" Henry asked.

"No, dummy," Janet rolled her eyes, "we can't."

"Why?"

"You know what?" Janet said. "This almost isn't worth it. If you hadn't touched him in the first place, none of this would be happening, Henry. None of it. I wouldn't be here worrying about how to get out of town ahead of schedule."

"But he saw me," Henry complained.

"Henry," Shane heard the woman sigh, and when she spoke again, it was in a tone of utter exasperation. "Okay, let me try and make this clear to you. He's alive. Someone will notice he is missing. They will come and look for him. They will find him and let him out. Most people won't believe a ghost hit him. But what if someone does? What if there is that one person out there who does? Are you going to want to go ahead and deal with Beverly?"

"No," Henry mumbled.

"No," Janet said. "I didn't think so."

"So, I got to kill 'm?" Henry asked.

"Yes, Henry," Janet said with exasperation, "you have to kill him."

Shane managed to get to his feet, taking in a ragged breath. *I'm going to kill you, Janet. Beverly too, whoever she is. First, Henry's going to get what he's got coming to him. Dead or not.*

"How do you want me to, huh?" Henry asked.

"I don't care," Janet said. "Really, Henry, I don't. I want you to go into the damned mausoleum and kill him. When you're done, you come out, and you tell me. Then we can all move on to the next town. Easy peasy, right?"

"Um, sure," Henry said. "Door's iron, Janet. How's I supposed to leave?"

For the first time, Shane saw the door to the mausoleum was slightly ajar. Using the wall as a support, he took a cautious step toward it, edging forward and wincing with every movement.

"I'll come and check on you tomorrow night," Janet said in an irritated tone. "I'm sure he'll be dead by then. Right?"

Oh, she's lying to you, Shane thought, smiling grimly. *She's not coming back for you. Not at all. You can hear it in her voice, Henry. She will be long gone once she closes the door. Cutting her losses because you're just too stupid.*

"Yup," Henry said chuckling. "Don't you worry none 'bout that, Janet. I'll kill 'm. It'll be fun. Ain't killed nobody in a long time."

"Double negatives, Henry," Janet muttered, and Shane smiled grimly.

Remember your grammar when I'm beating you to death,

Janet, Shane thought, and took another half-step toward the door. *Few more steps, that's it. Few more and I'll be right behind it.*

The temperature in the mausoleum plummeted, and the door slammed shut.

Shane stopped and listened. Old habits formed from twenty years with the Marines sprang to the surface. He didn't listen for breathing or movement. Instead, Shane waited. *He'll grab for me in a minute. Once he figures out I'm not where he left me.*

"She's stupid is what she is," Henry muttered, his voice coming from off to Shane's left. "If I'd a killed 'm, she and Beverly would be angry. Now I didn't kill 'm, she's still angry! What am I—hey, where you at?"

Silence followed. *He's waiting for me to answer him,* Shane realized. *He is seriously waiting for that. Damn, he IS dumber than a box of bricks.*

"Hey!" Henry yelled, the sound filling the mausoleum and driving through Shane's pounding head. "Answer me! Where you at?"

Something heavy fell to the floor, and a large crack resounded through the small structure.

Is he looking in the sarcophagi? Shane asked, dumbfounded.

Another crack, as stone met stone, answered his question.

This is unbelievable, Shane thought.

"I'm tellin' you now!" Henry bellowed. "Get out here, or I'm a whup you!"

Shane kept his mouth closed and reached out for the handle of the mausoleum's door only to discover there wasn't one. He reached higher, then lower, and was dismayed to find there was nothing to grasp.

No, there has to be a way to open it from the inside, Shane thought bitterly. *I just need time to find the damned thing!*

"Fella!" Henry yelled. "I heard you, come on now, playtime,

it's over!"

Shane bent down and sought a latch of any kind. Nothing met his hand.

"You by the door?" Henry asked, his voice moving closer. "Is that where you at?"

Shane's heartbeat quickened, increasing the pain in his head as he reached up, looking for a catch.

"Fella," Henry said. "I'm a kill you quick if you tell me where you at. If not, well, you ain't gunna like it. Not a bit, you won't."

Do not let me get killed by this idiot, Shane thought, dragging his hand down the seam of the iron door. He desperately searched for any type of catch.

Nothing met his fingers.

"You at the door, ain't you," Henry said softly. "Hell, you is. You tryin' to get out of here. Ain't nobody leavin' but me. Got it?"

Screw it, Shane thought. "Shut up. I'm trying to open this door, and I can't think with you crying back there."

"You can't talk to Henry like that!" the ghost bellowed.

"Great, third person," Shane said, dropping down to a sitting position.

Henry howled and, from what Shane could surmise, slammed into the iron door. For nearly a minute, the mausoleum was blissfully silent. It offered Shane enough time to light a cigarette and crawl over to his bag. He saw a sailor's folding knife on the floor, touched it, and felt an unnatural cold emanating from the steel and wood. Shane slid it to his bag and made himself comfortable.

"I know you're here," Henry said a moment later.

"I know you're stupid," Shane replied. "What prize do I get?"

"I'm a choke you to death, that's your prize," Henry snarled.

"Great, my favorite," Shane said, exhaling. "Tell you what. How about you go and get bent, and I'll pretend like you choked me. Sound good?"

"Shut up!" Henry roared.

"No, don't think so," Shane said. "Pretty sure you should just get out of here."

"Not 'til I kill you," Henry barked.

"Yeah, pretty convenient for your boss, huh?" Shane asked.

"What?" Henry demanded, a doubtful tone in his voice.

"Your boss," Shane continued. "I heard her, you know. Saying how she'd let you out tomorrow. Nice of you to believe that."

"She will," Henry declared, and the chill in the mausoleum increased.

"Sure she will," Shane said. "Like she said, though, you are dumber than a box of bricks."

There was a moment of hesitation, then Henry asked, "What are you sayin', fella?"

"What I'm saying," Shane said, "is, do you think she's really going to come back for you? You already messed up by not killing me, which I appreciate, by the way. But, on top of that, this doesn't seem like the first mistake you've made, big guy. So, I'll ask you. Do you really think she's coming back for you?"

"I'm a gunna kill you," Henry hissed.

"I believe you," Shane said. "I really do. That's why I'm going to ask a favor before you do it."

Henry hesitated, then asked, "What is it?"

"I've got two fifths of whiskey in my pack," Shane answered. "I'd like another cigarette and a drink before you finish me off."

"Whiskey," Henry said with longing. "Yeah. Drink up, fella. Heh, might make it hurt less when I kill you."

"It might at that," Shane said, chuckling. He rummaged around in his pack, found one of the fifths and withdrew it. Shane twisted off the cap, tossed it across the room and took a long pull from it.

"Is it good?" Henry asked.

"Oh, Henry," Shane said, snickering at his own, private joke, "it is magnificent. Nothing quite like a whiskey drunk."

"No," Henry sighed. "There ain't. Say, fella, how'd you get so ugly?"

"You're a sweetheart," Shane took a drag on his cigarette. "Let's see. I lost all my hair when I was a kid."

"You ain't got no hair at all?" Henry interrupted.

"None," Shane answered.

"What about all them scars? You in a accident or somethin'?" Henry asked.

"Battle scars, Henry my sweet," Shane said, taking another pull off the whiskey bottle. "Bullet wounds. Knife wounds. Frostbite. Lots of little memories."

"You a fighter, huh?" Henry asked.

"Marine," Shane answered. "Twenty-year man."

"Bare knuckles I was," Henry replied proudly. "Fighter in Philadelphia. Fought for the USS *Intrepid,* too, when I was a sailor."

"Huh," Shane said. He lit a fresh cigarette off the remnants of the old, rubbed the butt out and field-stripped it while he asked, "So, this your knife in here?"

"Yeah," Henry said, his tone shifting to that of a sulking child. "Janet threw it in. Make sure I finish the job before I get out."

"Why don't you just leave?" Shane asked, sliding his hand into his pack and finding a container of the table salt. He eased it out slowly, resting it between his legs as Henry answered the question.

"'Cause," Henry said bitterly. "Door's iron. Lock's iron. Can't open 'em up."

"I could do it," Shane offered, wincing as he touched Henry's knife and prying the blade out. He set the tool back on the floor, rubbing his hand against his jeans to warm the flesh.

"Nah," Henry said. "I have to kill you."

"Just because Janet said so?" Shane asked. He took another

drink.

"No. Well, yes," Henry sighed. "She'll tell Bev, and Bev, she's a rough lady. I knew a lady like her in Philly. Ran a cat house like she was a fella. Bev, she'll do me wrong. So, you know, I gotta listen to Janet."

"Sounds like a real peach," Shane said. Bracing himself, he used the knife to cut open the top of the salt container, saying, "So, how'd you die, champ?"

"In the cat house," Henry chuckled. "I was hired. Worked the door. Took care of fellas didn't know how's to act. Was a little rough with one of 'em. Broke his neck when I tossed him. His shipmates weren't too pleased. They come back a little later, stabbed me in the back."

"Huh," Shane said. He peeled the top away and sighed. "So, you're stuck with Janet and Bev now. Sure you don't want me to get you out of here?"

"Yeah," Henry said. "Thanks. You're not too bad, fella. Sorry, I gotta kill you. You ready yet?"

"Just about," Shane said, taking another drink. "Let me have a little more whiskey."

The dead man laughed. "You're a drinkin' man. I like that. Go ahead. Enjoy it."

"Thanks," Shane said, chuckling. "You know where you're headed next?"

"Nope," Henry said. "Never do. Well, not me, noways. They tell Chuck plenty, but I ain't afraid to say Chuck's a sight smarter 'n me."

"No, fooling?" Shane said. He repressed a hiss as he closed the knife.

"Yeah," Henry said. "'Bout ready?"

"Hm," Shane said, taking a deep breath. "Almost."

He picked up the knife and thrust it into the container of salt. Henry shouted as the mineral closed around his knife, dragging him back to it and trapping him there.

Shane sat and finished his cigarette as the temperature in the mausoleum gradually increased. He flicked his lighter open and held the flame over the makeshift salt prison. Nothing of the knife was visible. Shane carefully pushed the container away from him, sliding it into a tight corner. It wouldn't hold for long, he knew.

Long enough for me to take care of him later, Shane thought. He snapped the lighter closed and tucked it away. From his pack, he took out one of his sandwiches, unwrapped it and ate slowly, his head pounding. He washed the food down with more whiskey, lit another cigarette and then, painfully, stood up. Shane walked carefully forward, conscious of the damaged sarcophagi lying in the darkness.

After several minutes, he reached the door and sighed happily at the cool touch of iron beneath his fingers. He retrieved his lighter and used the flame to find the small latch which held the door closed. Chuckling, he freed the latch and pulled the door open.

Cool, fresh air touched his face, and the night sky shined with a full moon and brilliant stars.

"You're alive," Joan said, stepping cautiously out from the line of trees.

"Of course, I'm alive," Shane said, smiling. "Like the song says, 'ain't found a way to kill me yet.'"

"Where is he?" she asked, glancing nervously at the mausoleum.

"Sleeping," Shane said. "Or screaming. Who knows? Anyway, where are you buried?"

"Why?" Joan asked, confused.

"So we can get your necklace," Shane answered, lighting a fresh cigarette, "and get you back to your grandchildren."

* * *

71

Overnight Stay
By Sara Clancy

"Thank you for calling the front desk. This is Samantha, how can I help you?"

The well-practiced words didn't need any input from her brain to topple from her mouth. Off-season at The Ridge Hotel didn't really tax anyone mentally. And the night shift was all the worse. Samantha was on her second month of the graveyard shift. By this point, she only needed to skim the conversations for keywords. *Towels. Room-service. TV remote.* She was a little disappointed when the voice on the other end muttered 'towels'. It wasn't the least time consuming of all possible requests, but it was a close second.

She tuned in just enough to pick up how many towels were being requested and glanced at the phone screen to get the room number. Scribbling it all down in her note pad, she offered the standard send-off.

"Certainly. We'll be right with you. Have a lovely night."

Jabbing the tip of her pencil into the cradle, she hung up and started to dial housekeeping. She was one number off completing the task when she realized that she was throwing away a perfect opportunity to get out from behind the desk for a few minutes.

"You can handle the front desk on your own for a few moments, right? We don't have any more expected check-ins."

Caesar perked up, looking at her with wide, hopeful eyes. "What have you got?"

"Room 214 wants some towels," she said, slightly suspicious by his sudden burst of enthusiasm. "Since the room's so close, there's really no need to bother—"

"I'll go."

"But," Samantha said with a pout, "I took the call."

"Okay, okay, okay. But hear me out," he said. Pressing his hands together, he rested his chin on the tips of his fingers. "I'll annoy the hell out of you if you don't let me go."

"That's not fair."

He hummed contemplatively as he sucked in a deep breath. But, instead of an argument, he started singing 'What's New Pussycat'. There was a time when Samantha had liked the Tom Jones song. That was before her co-worker had started using it as verbal torture. There were only so many times anyone could stand to hear the same song on repeat before they broke.

"Fine! Just—stop, please."

Caesar dropped his hands. It irked her that he made absolutely no attempt to hide his victorious grin.

"I really want to hit you," she noted.

"Too bad you won't be able to reach me while I'm on the second floor," Caesar declared as he awkwardly threw himself over the high counter and started running.

Samantha sighed, retrieved a few towels from the Front Desk's stockpile, and met him with them when he sheepishly came back.

"Thank you," he mumbled.

Samantha kept her grip on the towels. "Bring me back something from the vending machine."

"Sure thing, partner."

"Really?"

"Yeah, of course." He was halfway across the foyer before calling out. "Oh, day shift didn't get to put any of today's check-ins into the computer system yet."

She glanced at the two piles of paperwork. "Which one have you started on?"

"Neither!" He declared as he bounded up the grand staircase.

She opened her mouth to protest, thought better of it, and huffed. Silence returned to the hotel lobby. It was broken only by the soft sounds of the crackling fireplace and the rapid clicking of the keyboard under her fingertips. Working steadily, she managed to get through half of the first pile before Caesar trotted back down the staircase. She didn't look up from the screen but reached out to take whatever treat he had given her. Instead, he flopped the towels onto the counter with all the limited dramatics the motion was able to create. Dropping his chin onto the pile, he stared at her until she asked.

"What's going on here?"

"You lied to me," he said.

"What are you going on about?"

"214, right?" he asked, continuing when she nodded. "No one answered the door. I think you inverted the numbers."

Her brow furrowed and she retrieved her notebook. While her handwriting was horrible, the numbers were clear enough.

"I'm sure that's what came up when they called," she mumbled.

"Did they say it or did you read it?" Caesar asked.

Uncertainty crept in and her frown deepened. "Hold on. Let me call them."

Cradling the phone between her shoulder and her ear, she quickly tapped in the few commands to bring up the phone's history log. At times like these, she was very grateful for the hotel's recent upgrade. For once, it hadn't just been aesthetics. It didn't take more than a few seconds for the phone to begin to ring in her ear. Caesar's sulking resonated in her other. Still slumped against the towels, he absently clicked his tongue. It was annoying.

She was attempting to shoo him away when the line clicked. Silence followed.

"Um, hello?" She shook her head and refocused. "This is Samantha from the front desk."

Silence.

"Is anyone there?"

"Samantha." Her name was said on a breath, low and soft. As if the speaker was struggling to work their mouth around the syllables.

"Yes, that's right."

Slowing her speaking pace, she motioned to Caesar that the guest had most likely been drinking. Not unusual. Most people up at this hour had been having a fun night.

"I'm so sorry to bother you," she continued, keeping her professional tone as Caesar rolled his eyes. "I just needed to quickly confirm that a request was made from this room number."

"*Samantha.*"

The whispered voice dragged her name out until it took almost ten seconds to get through it all. Biting her lips, she re-cradled the handset against her shoulder and searched for the reservation information for room 214 on the computer. The screen filled with the normal outline, but it was completely empty. *Come on, morning shift. Did you check anyone in?*

"Yes," she said again. "Can you confirm that you requested three towels for room 214?"

"*Yes.*"

The voice hissed the word and a chill worked its way down her spine.

"*Room 214. Bring us towels. Hurry.*"

"We'll be right there. Thank you and goodnight."

Hurriedly, she hung up the phone.

"Someone was in there, huh?" Caesar asked.

"Apparently."

"Then," he puffed out his cheeks, "why didn't they answer the door?"

"I don't know." The voice lingered in her head like an icy fog. Shaking herself once more, she sucked in a quick breath. "They said to hurry. Maybe they've clogged the sink or something."

"I guess I'll just head back up," Caesar said.

The rather undramatic reply was coupled with a heavy sigh and a long, slow slide that almost put him on the floor.

"I'll just stay here and do our jobs then," she called after him. "You do that."

She had started typing again before she remembered, "Don't forget my treat!"

He waved her off with a disgruntled huff at the top of the stairs before disappearing from sight. Everything fell silent once more. She worked through a few more of the check-ins before Caesar appeared at the top of the staircase. Instead of coming down, he stood there dramatically waving his arms until his black uniform shirt drew her attention. She looked up and, unwilling to scream across the foyer at midnight, settled for a little dramatics of her own, exaggerating a confused shrug. He pointed to the towels then back down the hallway. *They still won't answer.*

"They've definitely been drinking then," she muttered with some annoyance and snatched up the phone again.

Before she had a chance to dial, she thought better of it. None of the surrounding guests would be all that pleased to have their neighbor's phone blaring so late at night. Once they might overlook. Twice would be too much. She set the phone back and met Caesar's gaze. It was a lot harder to mime 'leave it at their door' than she had expected. Between them, it took about five minutes for them to get on the same page. And that was only because she snatched up a notebook and wrote 'leave it' in large lettering.

Once he got the message, things went rather smoothly, and he was bouncing back across the foyer.

"Did you get my snack?" Samantha asked without looking up from the computer monitor.

He spun on his heel and left once more. Two more check-ins

and a small bag of spicy potato chips smacked against her forehead.

"Sorry, I was aiming for your shoulder," Caesar grinned.

"Just for that, you don't get any." She chuckled in the face of his righteous indignation as the phone rang. One hand kept typing in the guest information while the other retrieved the phone.

"Thank you for calling the front desk. This is Samantha, how can I help you?"

"*Samantha.*"

Ice crackled around her spine, making her snap upright. Caesar noticed the change and gave her a questioning look. It was enough for her to realize how silly she was being. *It's just a drunk guest. Get it together.*

"Hello again. We seem to keep missing each other. We left them outside for you."

"*You didn't come.*"

"I assure you, the towels are just outside your door," she said.

"*You didn't come.*" The words crackled around the edges like spitting fire.

"What is it?" Caesar asked.

She cupped her hand over the mouthpiece. "They're saying that you never went up."

He spun around to fling his arms towards the stairs, the motion screaming 'you saw me!'

"I believe you," she said.

It unnerved her that the guest of room 214 was yet to reply. The other end of the line was just a deep, unbroken silence. Not even the slight shuffle of noise that came when someone hung up. Just—nothing.

"Are they high?" Caesar asked.

She shot him a glare, motioning that the person in question was still on the line. If the guest heard, they didn't comment.

"Just hang up," Caesar said.

"I can't do that," she whispered back before returning her attention to the guest. "Hello? Have you checked outside your door?"

"*Room 214.*"

"Yes, that's right. That's where we left them for you."

"Samantha," Caesar hissed, slumping against the counter and waving his other hand to get her attention. "Hang up."

'No' she mouthed, once more disturbed by the consuming nothingness seeping from the handset.

"Either they're an idiot," Caesar continued. "Or they've partied way too hard to remember any of this in the morning. So..." He let the sentence trail off in favor of miming hanging up the phone.

She huffed and reluctantly nodded.

"Hello?"

Silence.

"The towels have been delivered to room 214. Have a wonderful night."

There was no reply and she quickly hung up. Staring at the phone for a moment, she looked up at her co-worker.

"If I get in trouble for that, you've got my back, right?"

"Yeah, sure." He dismissed, slithering his torso across the top of the counter and wiggling his eyebrows at the bag of chips. "For a price."

The phone rang again. He flopped one arm down to blindly snatch it up.

"Thank you for calling the front desk. This is Caesar; how can I help you?"

She opened the bag and dramatically munched on the first chip, watching with amusement as his face distorted in mock outrage. The expression didn't last long and soon crumbled into something she couldn't quite interpret.

"No, my name is Caesar. I can help you, though. What do you need?"

"What's going on?" She whispered.

He waved her off.

"She's just gone on break," he told the caller. "But I can help you. Is there something you need?"

Samantha glanced at the phone's display screen. Room 214.

"Right. I'll put you through to room service, have a lovely evening."

Caesar leaned heavily on the counter to transfer the call.

"What a weirdo," he said as he returned the handset. "Side question; is that a dude or a dudette?"

It occurred to her then that she hadn't been able to determine anything from the voice. It was utterly void of markers that would generally supply information: tone, accent, tempo, or anything of the like.

She shrugged. "What did they want?"

"You."

Dread tickled to form a pool in the pit of her stomach. "What?"

"They just kept saying your name," he forced a teasing smile. "Maybe they have a crush."

She rolled her eyes, which only provoked Caesar.

"Oh, don't you see. They heard your melodious voice and fell helplessly in love. Smitten but shy, they sit alone in their room, staring at the only connection they have to you. The phone."

"That just sounds creepy."

"Yeah, it really does, doesn't it?" He winced.

"So, you sent them to room service?"

He shrugged one shoulder. "They said the magic word, 'food'. Which means they're not our problem anymore."

Caesar, seemingly having decided that he was either too bored or too good for doors, once against opted to scurry over the table instead of going around. What few tasks they had were put aside for the time it took to eat the bag of chips, each one teasing the other for the inability to handle the heat. Then the phone rang.

They both looked to the display, releasing a long sigh when they discovered that it wasn't room 214. Samantha dreaded to hear that voice again. The way it hissed her name. Surprised by how horrified she was by the thought of room 214 reaching out again, she gladly answered this call.

"Hey, Seth. What's up?"

"Who the hell is in room 214?"

Samantha cringed. *You can't bill a guest until they're in the system.* "I don't know. Our paperwork's a little behind."

"But they're a freak," Caesar called playfully, crowding closer to share the phone. "Hey dude, can you swing by a soda on your way up?"

"I'll be up to date soon," she promised, trying to shove Caesar away and collect her notebook at the same time. "Just keep a tab and I'll apply the charges. What did they order?"

"Nothing," Seth said. "Sammy, they just kept asking for you. Do you know them or something?"

Caesar pulled back just far enough to study her out of the corner of his eyes.

"No," she said.

Caesar's eyebrow lifted a little higher.

"I know protocol. If they were a guest of mine, I'd have put it in the system."

Shrugging one shoulder in recognition, Caesar pushed back into her personal space to share the phone once again.

"So, they didn't order anything?" Caesar asked.

"All they'd say was their room number and Samantha's name," Seth answered.

His voice carried all the unspoken anxiety Samantha felt. It didn't matter how many times she told herself she was overreacting, there was no shaking the feeling that something was very wrong. Caesar quickly caught Seth up on the whole problem with the towels, ending with a concerned look and whispered, "Maybe we should let security know."

"But they haven't been belligerent or inappropriate," Samantha replied. "I can't just Red List them because I find them creepy."

"I can," Seth said. "That's one of the great things about being a manager."

Samantha chewed her bottom lip. She must have released a nervous little sigh because Seth was quick to add.

"Sammy, they asked for you. *Only you.* Either you've given them the best customer service of their life, or they're trying to get you alone. Their ass is on the Red List. No one's to go up there by themselves. Got it?"

Samantha and Caesar agreed in unison and the conversation ended swiftly after that. Once she hung up, she started hurriedly looking through the remaining stack of paperwork, searching for room 214.

"Are you sure you don't know this person?" Caesar asked.

Samantha shook her head rapidly.

"Hey, it's okay," Caesar said, placing a hand on her shoulder. "Look, I bet they just had one too many and remembered the cute girl at front desk. Remember that guy a few months ago?"

"The creep that ordered room service just to answer the door without pants on?" She continued to flip through the pages, but now at a far slower pace.

"Yeah," he smirked. "You should have seen his face when Seth and I went up instead of Grace."

"You've said that numerous times," she said with a small smile.

"Well, I bet this person is just like that. Someone gross that's physically harmless. They'll pass out soon enough and that'll be the end of it."

She nodded, now slowly flicking through the last of the stack. Caesar looped his arm around her shoulders and gave her a reassuring squeeze.

"Hey, if they call again, I'm answering. Got it? You've gone home for the night. Replaced by Donny, a hairy bodybuilder that believes deodorant is a trick by big pharma."

A giggle escaped her and he threw his arms up in victory.

"Thanks," she said as he danced around in celebration. "It's just late. I'm being paranoid."

"This place can wig you out."

Unstable silence pushed in at the end of his sentence. For a moment, they stood there, feeling it press down upon them. It felt different somehow. Colder even as the fireplace made the room border on stifling. Dark even as the overhead lights glistened off of the polished wood that surrounded them. There was something about the night that just felt wrong. They both flinched when the log on the fire gave a loud, sudden pop. Caesar chuckled nervously and rubbed the back of his neck.

"I need coffee. What about you? Creamer, no sugar, right?"

She nodded her thanks and, almost absentmindedly, continued through the last few pages. Perhaps it was her fatigue, but she almost passed by the very sheet she was looking for. *Room 214,* she read. *Wayne Rossie.* She studied the attached sheets. Every guest was required to show identification upon check-in. Normally, it was only so they could cross-check the general information with the credit card provided. But, when the guest requested the use of a parking space, the front desk kept a photocopy.

She stared at the small photograph, trying to recall a moment when their paths had crossed. It wasn't any use. After a while, the constant procession of guests blended together. Wayne was neither remarkable enough nor repugnant enough to stick in her memory. Shoulder-length dark hair, slightly tanned skin, full lips, and dark eyes.

"Oh, hey, is that him?" Caesar asked, suddenly appearing over her shoulder and making her jump.

"Don't do that."

"Sorry," he offered her coffee in apology. "But is that him? Wayne. Nah, I don't remember him. When did he check in?"

She flicked back to the front page. "Seven-thirty tonight."

"So... we were the ones to check him in?"

"I guess so."

"How come he's not in the system then?"

She arched an eyebrow at him. "Gee, I wonder which one of us checked him in."

Caesar quickly changed the subject. "See, I told ya. He's just a socially awkward, lonely guy. Nothing to worry about."

She took a sip of her drink to avoid replying, remembering a little too late that the coffee machine was set to scalding. Stifling a pained gasp, she leaned forward, caught somewhere between spitting the boiling mouthful out and choking it down. The sharp motion made the liquid slosh over the rim and burned her fingers.

"Hey, you okay?" Caesar asked.

"Yeah," she hissed.

"Go put it under water. I've got this."

She thanked him and fled for the nearest bathroom while her hand throbbed with pain. It was only once she had it under the icy faucet that she realized she had unthinkingly gone up to the second floor — the public restroom situated just down the hallway from room 214.

"Stupid."

It was a word that she thought accurately described herself and her actions over the last few minutes. Still, she stayed until the sharp pain turned into an aching numbness. Taking a moment to fix her hair, she straightened her uniform top and opened the bathroom door.

"*Samantha.*" The raspy voice whispered into her ear.

Choking on a gasp, she spun, smacking against the doorframe. She rubbed her shoulder and looked around, trying to pinpoint where the sound had come from. The hallway was empty. The hotel quiet.

"Stupid girl," she whispered to herself as her scanning gaze settled on the door of room 214.

A deep chill slithered along her spine and she suppressed a shiver. Wrapping her arms around herself, she set off to the nearby staircase.

"*Samantha.*"

She stopped short. Not just because of Wayne's whisper, but because of the metallic click that followed. She turned towards a dull rasp. The door to 214 slowly opened, inch by inch, revealing the darkness that lingered within the room. It was impossible to make out anything within the ebony. Even the hallway light couldn't creep more than an inch into the room before being cut off with a razor's edge. The long, slithering voice coiled out from the abyss, calling for her once again.

Samantha sprinted for the staircase. She raced down the steps, not looking back until she was in the foyer and in clear view of the front desk. Walking backward, she stared at the top of the staircase, waiting to see Wayne following her. He didn't. The staircase remained empty. The world around her stilled. It was the quiet that caught her off guard and she looked over to the front desk. Surely Caesar should have more than enough to tease her by this point. He wasn't there.

A fizzle, a pop, and the hallway above her dimmed. She looked up just as the sound came again. Another lightbulb shattered, allowing the night to encroach a little further. She flinched as the bulb died. Glass fragments scattered across the top of the staircase as darkness descended. It dropped like a curtain, thick and opaque, to cover the entire landing. It didn't matter that the remaining lights still blazed with a near sterile glare. The wall of shadows remained, cutting the world off after the top stair.

She fled, unable to turn her back on the incredible sight. Caesar still hadn't reappeared as she threw herself through the door into the front desk's back office. The self-locking door clicked into place as she pressed herself against it, determined not to be seen from the foyer. Still, she snuck a peek, relieved to see the familiar brilliance of the polished lobby.

She slumped, thumped the back of her head against the door, and chastised herself for being so easily startled. The spike of panic that had propelled her to run now withered, allowing her brain to think up a flood of excuses for what she had just seen. *I need to call maintenance.* But all the bravado she had built up proved to be a fragile thing. She couldn't bring herself to leave her makeshift hiding spot. So, instead of going to the phone, she decided her first task was to figure out where Caesar had gone. A pair of wall-mounted monitors displayed the security camera feed; four little black and white pictures to each screen. She glanced across them. *Not outside. Not in the bar getting another coffee. Not in the downstairs hallway.* Samantha's lungs froze into hard lumps. The square that should have displayed the upstairs hallway was completely black.

"Well, yeah," she told herself, just to hear a voice in the silence. "The light's out."

Her gaze flicked to the monitor displaying the foyer. The impenetrable darkness still swelled at the top of the stairs. As she watched, it bulged and bled. It moved like ooze, reluctantly giving up the figure that walked out of its depths.

The silhouette of a tall, narrow man stalked slowly down the staircase. Each stride purposeful but jolting. There wasn't any color to him. No definition between skin and hair and clothes.

Just a living shadow. It traveled down the staircase and, at last, moved beyond the reach of the camera. Samantha hurriedly shifted her gaze to the next monitor. The shadow was there. Still moving in a shuffling gait. Drifting ever closer to the front desk. She watched it cross the foyer, untouched and unchanged by the overhead lights and flickering fire. Silence bombarded her. The absence of footsteps thrilling her more than a heavy stride could have.

"*Samantha,*" the haunting voice whispered from the foyer. "*Come to me.*"

She clamped a hand over her mouth to keep her silence.

The voice took on a sharper edge. "*Samantha. Come here.*"

Watching the monitor, seeing the dark shape standing before the check-in, she gripped the door with her free hand. Her muscles twitched as adrenaline flooded her veins. Cold sweat slicked her palms, but she promised herself, if it was to touch the desk, she would run. *To the bar! People are still in the bar.* It seemed a million miles away.

"*Samantha!*" The voice boomed, rattling the items scattered across her work desk. Her pen rolled from her notebook to clatter against the floor. "*Room 214! Come now!*"

The voice cut into her like a razor. By the monitor, she watched the figure press against the counter, bleeding into it. A new wave of terror flooded over her as the hissing voice turned into a distorted purr.

"*I'm waiting for you, Samantha. I'll always be waiting.*"

The door slammed against her back, throwing her onto the thin carpet of the back office. She screamed, scrambling away, unsure where to go to hide.

"Samantha?" Caesar crouched down next to her, grabbing her shoulders, his wide eyes struggling to grab her scattered gaze. "Sammy, it's me. You're okay."

She flinched as sound flooded back into her world. A stream

of people moved across the foyer, the motion marked by repeating bursts of red and blue lights. Something smacked down against the counter and she yelped.

"It's okay," Caesar rapidly assured.

A few rapid blinks and the dark figure she dreaded turned to a uniformed police officer. *They're all police officers.*

"What's going on?" she asked.

"Where have you been?" Caesar asked. "You scared the hell out of me when I couldn't find you."

"I went upstairs. The bathroom. Where were you? What's happening?"

"Is she okay?" The officer asked.

"I think so," Caesar said.

"Ma'am, did you have an interaction with Wayne Rossie?" The officer asked.

"She was here when I checked him in," Caesar answered while Samantha gathered her senses.

"He also requested that I bring up some towels."

"It's lucky that you didn't," Another officer said as he approached his co-worker. The police lowered their voices to a series of whispers, leaving them time for Caesar to help Samantha to her feet.

"They're here looking for Wayne," Caesar hurriedly told her. "They came just after you left. Why didn't you go to the downstairs bathroom?"

She looked at him, dumbfounded. "Why are they looking for him?"

Caesar looked to the officer that was now calling them over. "Probably best that he explains."

Samantha didn't feel the steps it took to meet the man at the desk. The man asked a series of simple questions. The well-known answers didn't need any input from her brain to topple from her mouth. It left her adrift as the officer divulged carefully selected information.

"Wayne Rossie is wanted in connection with a series of murders. His modus operandi is to check into hotels under a fake name. He then calls down with a request to lure someone to his room."

Samantha's brain surged into motion to fill in what the man had neglected to say.

"He intended to kill me?"

"But he was under his real name," Caesar said.

The office nodded, "We were closing in on him. I suspect this was to be a last hurrah of sorts." Catching himself, he cleared his throat and returned to the facts. "You're very lucky. We suspect he had a stroke just after calling you."

"But he called again! He talked to Caesar. To Seth—" She continued even as Caesar explained who Seth was. "He followed me down here."

"Ma'am, first examinations estimate he's been dead for hours."

Samantha rocked on her feet, only keeping upright as Caesar caught her. *I'm waiting for you. I'll always be waiting for you.* She tipped her head up to meet her friend's eyes.

"I quit."

* * *

If you enjoyed the book, please leave a review. Your reviews inspire us to continue writing about the world of spooky and untold horrors!

Check out these best-selling books from our talented authors

Ron Ripley (Ghost Stories)
- Berkley Street Series Books 1 – 9
  www.scarestreet.com/berkleyfullseries
- Moving in Series Box Set Books 1 – 6
  www.scarestreet.com/movinginboxfull

A. I. Nasser (Supernatural Suspense)
- Slaughter Series Books 1 – 3 Bonus Edition
  www.scarestreet.com/slaughterseries

David Longhorn (Sci-Fi Horror)
- Nightmare Series: Books 1 – 3
  www.scarestreet.com/nightmarebox
- Nightmare Series: Books 4 – 6
  www.scarestreet.com/nightmare4-6

Sara Clancy (Supernatural Suspense)
- Banshee Series Books 1 – 6
  www.scarestreet.com/banshee1-6

For a complete list of our new releases and best-selling horror books, visit www.scarestreet.com/books

See you in the shadows,
Team Scare Street

Made in the USA
Monee, IL
24 October 2024

68586817R00056